DATE DUE

			Demco

PLAYING ATARI
with SADDAM HUSSEIN

PLAYING ATARI
with
SADDAM HUSSEIN

Based on a True Story

Jennifer Roy with Ali Fadhil

HOUGHTON MIFFLIN HARCOURT
BOSTON NEW YORK

www.hmhco.com

The text was set in Adobe Caslon Pro.
Title page art © 2018 by Patrick Leger
Map art © 2018 by Lucy Banaji

Library of Congress Cataloging-in-Publication Data
Names: Roy, Jennifer Rozines, 1967– author. |
Fadhil, Ali, joint author.
Title: Playing Atari with Saddam Hussein : based on a real life story
/ Jennifer Roy and Ali Fadhil
Description : Boston ; New York : Houghton Mifflin Harcourt,
[2018] | Summary: For forty-two days in 1991, eleven-year-old
Ali Fadhil and his family struggle to survive as Basra, Iraq,
is bombed by the United States and its allies.
Identifiers: LCCN 2016057657 | ISBN 9780544785076
Subjects: LCSH: Persian Gulf War, 1991—Juvenile fiction. |
CYAC: Persian Gulf War, 1991—Fiction. | Family Life—Iraq—
Fiction. | Hussein, Saddam, 1937–2006—Fiction. | Iraq—
History—20th century—Fiction.
Classification: LCC PZ7.R812185 PI 2018 |DDC [Fic]—dc23
LC record available at https://lccn.loc.gov/2016057657

Manufactured in the United States of America
DOC 10 9 8 7 6 5 4 3 2 1
4500691129

To the good people of Iraq.
—J.R.

To the brave men and women of the United
States Armed Forces: THANK YOU!
—A.F.

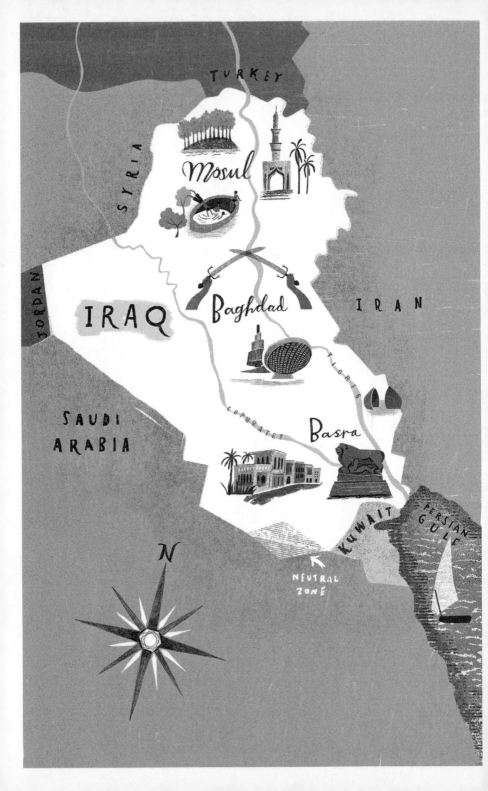

BASRA, IRAQ,
1991

ONE

THE AFTERNOON THE BOMBS START FALLING, I GET MY highest score ever on my favorite video game.

"Boys!" Mama yells. "It's time!"

I ignore her, too busy taunting my brother Shirzad.

"I am the champion of the universe!" I tell him. Shirzad reaches out, trying to grab the controller from my hand. But I don't let him have it. Not yet. First I need to put my name up as the high score.

A-L-I. I maneuver the stick and buttons and then hit Enter. My brother's initials drop down to second place.

"Give me that," Shirzad grumbles. "It's my turn and I'm going to take you down."

"Boys! What is wrong with you?" Mother appears in the doorway. "Put that garbage away and get to the safe room. It's almost time for the war." She turns and is gone.

The war. It's really here. The adults have been talking

about it for weeks and weeks. It had seemed about as real as the virtual war I was just playing onscreen.

Until now. The United Nations deadline for Iraq's withdrawal from Kuwait has expired. It's time for war.

I throw the controller into the box that holds all our game stuff. Shirzad shuts down the Atari console.

"Race you," he says, and takes off running. I'm right behind him. It's hard to run on the tile floor when I'm just wearing socks, and just before we reach the "safe room" I slip and slide. I crash into my brother and we land in a heap on the floor.

Right at the feet of our father.

"What kind of example are you setting for your younger brother and sister?" he says. "Stand up and stop acting like animals."

"Yes, Baba," we say together.

Shirzad and I get up. At the last moment, Shirzad stretches his longer legs and steps ahead of me into the room.

"I win," he whispers to me. But it's a hollow victory, because the first person in the safe room is the first person Mama puts to work. She tells Shirzad to help Baba move the bed away from the window.

I'm tasked to shut the remaining windows and close the curtains. I go over to a window that looks over the side yard. Baba has already removed the metal air conditioner from the window. If a bomb hits nearby, flying glass will be bad enough, but a flying air conditioner would be worse. A warm breeze is blowing in. Even in January, the weather is mild.

The sun has set. I can still discern the outlines of the date and palm trees in the yard and the gray stone privacy wall that surrounds our house. Beyond the wall is our city of Basra, wrapped in an eerie silence, waiting.

"Mama!" My younger sister, Shireen, bursts into the room. "When will the war start?"

"They said on the radio it will start sometime during the night," Mama says. "Where is Ahmed? He was just here."

"I'm back," my younger brother says, careening into the room. "Shireen made me go get this heavy basket. What's in here, anyway—rocks?"

"No, it's a picnic," Shireen says. "Flatbread, tomatoes, olives, hummus, and Coca-Colas. And date cookies for dessert."

A picnic for a war? Shireen is only six. She doesn't really remember what war is like. I'm eleven, and I know all too well. This is already my second war.

I go around shutting the windows. Normally, at this hour we kids would be getting ready for bed. It should be a school night, not a war night.

"Ahmed," says Mama. "Stop fooling around." Ahmed is

clutching a small rolled-up rug, running into the wall and bouncing off. *Run! Bash! Fall!* He comes to a halt and walks over to a pile of small rugs stacked against the wall.

My job is done, so I go over and help Ahmed lay the rugs around the room. Five rugs for Mama and four kids. One bed for my father.

"I still can't believe that we are at war with the United States of America," Ahmed says. "What could Saddam be thinking?"

"For sure he is not thinking about his own people," I say.

TWO

SADDAM HUSSEIN IS THE PRESIDENT OF IRAQ. GEORGE Bush is the president of the United States. The United States of America is the most powerful country in the world. Iraq, my country, is the most foolish.

Last August, five months ago, Saddam ordered our army to invade a neighboring country, Kuwait. Everyone knows you can't just go and take over someone else's country. But my president did it anyway.

So President George Bush and a bunch of other world leaders have formed a coalition to stop Saddam and take back Kuwait. Iraq is an ant compared to this coalition. They will crush us like a bug.

"I hate Saddam," my sister, Shireen, says loudly. "He's ruining my life."

"Shhh . . ." My parents shush her. What Shireen said would be amusing if it weren't so important to be cautious.

Yes, we are inside our house, among family. But we were taught to never speak against Saddam Hussein.

He is evil. If he heard what my little sister just said about him, he would probably cut out her tongue. Or his henchmen would do it for him.

Saddam's people are everywhere. One of the members of his government lives on our street. We have to be extra careful. A cloud of paranoia hangs over our neighborhood games.

"Children," Baba says. "Find a place away from the windows and settle down."

I claim an orange and brown striped rug and lay it out next to Shirzad's gray one. The younger kids sit closer to my parents. I have two brothers and a sister. It goes: Shirzad, me, Ahmed, Shireen.

We all have dark hair, olive skin, and big brown eyes. My siblings look like a mix of both sides of our family. But me? I am a copy of my mother. I look like my mother in boy form.

People remark on the resemblance all the time. "Your son," they'll say to Mama, "he's exactly like you!"

"On the outside, yes," my mother will respond. Serious and stoic, she is a respected professor of mathematics.

I hate math. And school in general.

We went to school most days during the last war. This

war? School has been canceled! At least something good has come from the mess Saddam has created.

"Hey!" I've been hit by a rolled-up sock. A smelly sock. I throw it back at Ahmed, who is laughing like a lunatic. Normally, I'd jump him and wrestle him to the ground, but I see my father's frown.

Baba is almost as strict as Mama—his patients love him, but they only see the pleasant, easygoing professional who takes care of their teeth. During the day, my father works his mandatory government job as a dentist. In the evening, he does orthodontics at his own clinic for private clients. He fills cavities for the poor and puts braces on the wealthy.

Baba left his small rural town in northern Iraq and worked his way through university and dental school.

"I came from nothing and made myself into something," he tells us over and over. He calls us kids lazy and spoiled and soft. It's true, we don't have to work like he did. Until recently we had nannies and a gardener and a cook to do all the work for us.

Except for schoolwork. It makes my parents crazy. They expect us to get all As. None of us are A students, but I'm the worst.

My attitude is, why spend time memorizing dates and doing math problems when the world is crumbling around us?

My attitude is not appreciated.

There is one class, however, in which I do get As. English.

My English teachers think it's because of them that I'm so good with the language. But really, my best English teacher is the television.

I'm obsessed with American TV shows. We have one channel that shows them, with Arabic subtitles. Turn that channel on and I'm like a sponge, absorbing American English. My favorite programs are the westerns, but I like the detective shows nearly as much. Everything about America fascinates me—the food, the celebrities, the freedom.

"Enough!" My father is breaking up a kicking fight between Ahmed and Shireen. Only Ahmed gets yelled at, as usual. Shireen is spoiled, just as Baba says, and she gets away with everything.

I look around at my family and feel the walls closing in. Oh, how I wish I had been born in a different place, where people are happy and carefree.

Where families are not in hiding, hoping to live through the night. For no other reason except their leader is a madman.

I go to my rug and sit down.

I could be brave. After all, this isn't my first war. I survived that one, didn't I? But I am not stupid. Luck can run out at any time; worlds can be destroyed in an instant. I am scared. I am powerless and I feel betrayed.

Soon, America — the land that I love — is going to try to kill me. I'll try not to take it personally.

THREE

THURSDAY, JANUARY 17, 1991—DAY 2

HOURS PASS. BABA IS RESTLESS. HE FIDDLES WITH THE radio, trying to get the latest news. Finally he settles on one station.

The younger kids have dozed off, with Mama sitting silently near them.

Shirzad is humming to himself. I pick at a stray thread on my rug.

"This is the Voice of America!" a newscaster blares from the battery-powered radio, waking up Ahmed and Shireen and making me jump. "The air campaign is under way. Coalition planes have reached Baghdad."

Shireen lets out a wail. "They said Baghdad," Ahmed retorts scornfully. "We're in *Basra*. Dummy."

"I know that, *dummy*." Shireen kicks Ahmed.

Mama comforts Shireen and scolds Ahmed.

"Shush!" Baba says. The Voice of America drones on about the planes that are cutting a swath through western Iraq to get to Baghdad, our capital city.

Our relatives live in Baghdad—aunts, uncles, cousins. We visit them a couple times a year. I think Baghdad is too big and too dirty, crowded and unsafe.

My city, Basra, is smaller and farther south. It's in the desert, so it's hot, but the Tigris and the Euphrates Rivers meet and flow through it, adding a stripe of blue to the tans and browns of the desert. Basra is edged by swamps, so when my cousins visit they complain about the 'swamp stink.' I'm so used to it, I don't notice any smell. I think my cousins are jealous because Baghdad's such a pit. Still, I hope it isn't damaged too badly. I hope my relatives are okay.

Right now, Basra's biggest problem is not its swamps. It's that our city is only thirty miles from Kuwait's border.

Kuwait is a country that borders us to the south. The main route from Baghdad to Kuwait runs right through Basra.

"Who cares about Kuwait, anyway?" I whisper to Shirzad. "It's a tiny speck on the globe."

"A speck full of oil," Shirzad replies.

"Yeah." I sigh. Saddam wants to take Kuwait's oil, worth billions of dollars. The money likely won't be used to feed our people, but to feed his ego. He wants the world to think he's the greatest, the most powerful. Sometimes I think our president is like Shireen, always trying to get attention from the big kids.

In my lifetime, we have barely had any peace. Our last war was with Iran, and it dragged on for eight years. Eight years! It began when I was one year old and ended when I was nine. And nobody even won.

So now what does Saddam Hussein do? He sends our army to invade Kuwait.

Which is against all international rules, and the reason that group of countries has formed an alliance to get Saddam out of Kuwait and to punish him. Not just any group of countries. The United States of America plus Britain, Syria, Canada, France, Italy, Egypt, Qatar, Saudi Arabia, Bahrain, and the United Arab Emirates, plus a bunch more. The news said thirty-four countries, the largest coalition since World War Two. All teamed up against us. And Saddam still thinks this was a good idea?

We're doomed, I think to myself, for perhaps the thousandth time. We regular Iraqis are here just trying to live our lives, but now we could be bombed?

A voice on the radio is saying something about American "smart bombs," with technology for "pinpoint accuracy" in taking out military targets. These smart bombs are designed to reduce "collateral casualties," which means the Americans will do their best not to kill innocent people. At least this is what American radio says.

I look at Shirzad, and say the last words either of us will be able to hear for a while.

"I hope those bombs are as smart as they claim."

My brother nods. I know we are thinking the same thing. The more accurate the bombs, the less likely we are to die.

And then we hear it. A spooky whistling sound in the distance, followed by a *boom*.

It is zero hour.

The war has arrived.

FOUR

IMAGINE AN EARTHQUAKE. IT RATTLES YOUR HOUSE, and things fall off shelves.

That would be like the war with Iran.

Now imagine another earthquake. The ground beneath you shakes violently, knocking you off your feet. You lie helpless on the floor as the world roars and rages around you.

That would be like our first night at war with America.

Bombs.

Many, many bombs.

Raining down on our city.

My ears are clogged with the sounds of explosions and sirens and my mother's prayers: "God, please protect my family," over and over.

I think I am most frightened about my mother, because she does not even believe in God. I flatten myself on the floor and hope our safe room is really safe, considering it's just my brother Shirzad's bedroom.

"Why *my* room?" Shirzad had protested when my parents first told him about its new use.

"Don't be selfish," Baba said. "Your room is farthest away from the high school." That shut Shirzad up.

One might wonder what a high school has to do with war. But that is how President Saddam's twisted mind works. He places weapons on the roofs of school buildings, hospitals . . . anywhere innocent civilians may be, so he can use them as human shields. When the enemy tries to destroy military capabilities, including these improvised ones, like schools and hospitals, well, that's when Saddam goes on TV and says, "Look how evil our enemies are—killing children and sick people!"

The military has put an antiaircraft weapon on the roof of our local high school. Which is only *two blocks* from our house. The weapon can shoot at enemy fighter jets overhead. Of course those planes can fire back. And drop bombs. So, this antiaircraft weapon on top of the high school makes our neighborhood a target. Our street might as well have a bull's-eye with Saddam Hussein's face on it.

War is no joke, and the coalition that's attacking us is not kidding. The bombs and guns and sirens are relentless. Our house is shaking so hard that I'm scared it might collapse. And then—

The power goes out. It's so dark, I can't even see Shirzad. In a room filled with family, I feel alone.

Terror. Noise. Both keep me awake, frozen flat on the floor. Thoughts of death poke at the corners of my brain, but I won't let them in. Instead I start to make a list in my head of things that I like.

Dolma grape leaves stuffed with meat and rice and spices. Chicken soup. Baklava pastry with chopped nuts and honey . . . yum. No more food. What else do I like? My Superman comics collection. Beating Shirzad at anything. My country . . .

Suddenly I feel a rush of emotion for Iraq. *Not* the Iraq of Saddam Hussein, but the true Iraq, the one every student learns about in history class. The ancient civilizations of Sumer and Mesopotamia were built on our soil, where the first cities were created and where the wheel and the oldest known system of writing — cuneiform — were invented. My mother likes to point out that Mesopotamians developed the "base ten" math we use today, the sixty-second minute, the sixty-minute hour, the first calendar . . . and the first schools.

Did I mention my mother is a math teacher?

Iraq was once called Babylon, whose hanging gardens were one of the Seven Wonders of the World.

And now all that history is being bombed to bits.

Reality strikes a dagger into my heart, and the fear that I've been trying so hard to stave off floods my being.

Thinking about how great Iraq used to be is making me sad. And right behind the sadness is fear. *I'm so scared so-scaredsoscared . . .*

Just as I'm about to start crying, a tune that always makes me happy sneaks its way into my mind. So I start to sing, quietly at first . . .

"It's time to start the music.

"It's time to light the lights.

"It's time to meet the Muppets

"On the *Muppet Show* tonight!"

My voice grows stronger and louder, as I picture Kermit and Fozzie Bear and Miss Piggy. And crazy Animal, bashing away on his drum set.

And then I hear them, my brothers and my sister, loud enough to drown out the bombs.

"It's time to get things started on the most sensational inspirational celebrational Muppetational . . . this is what we call 'the *Muppet Show!*'"

BOOM!

A bomb hits so close, my teeth vibrate. I curl up into a little ball, as small as I can make myself, and think of nothing.

FIVE

WE SURVIVED THE NIGHT.

Our house was not hit. My family is alive. As the sun comes up, we hear a welcome sound. It's the "all clear" siren. There will be no more attacks, for now.

"Let's go outside and look around!" Ahmed says. Shirzad and I created this tradition from our last war. The morning after an attack we went on an adventure hunt, searching for damage. We had told Ahmed about it and now he would come along, too.

But this was very different from the war with Iran. Back then, after a night of fighting we might find a hole in a building or rubble on the road. I didn't want to imagine what it was like outside now.

"Not quite yet," Baba says. "Let's listen to what the radio has to say." Baba turns the radio up full volume, just in time for us to hear the voice of Saddam Hussein.

"The great duel, the mother of all battles has begun!" Saddam declares. "The dawn of victory nears as this great showdown begins!"

Baba clicks the radio off.

"I've heard enough," he grumbles.

"Did we win?" Shireen asks.

We all look at her. How do you explain state propaganda to a six-year-old? Saddam is famous for spinning the news to make himself look good.

"No, we haven't won," Shirzad says. "Yet."

I reach out and punch him in the arm. He jumps on me and we start wrestling.

"Boys!" Mama says sharply.

"No, Khawlah, let them be children," Baba says. "They'll be men soon enough."

That stops me mid-punch. In a few years, Shirzad will be old enough to be a soldier—and then I'll be too. If Saddam says we are at war, all men aged eighteen and over must fight. I don't know what I want to be when I grow up, but it's definitely not a soldier.

Shirzad gets up and pulls me upright alongside him. Soon we are all standing and stretching out the stiffness we acquired from a night on the floor.

A part of me still feels shook up, but I push that part deep inside me. We survived. In war, that's what matters.

"I have to work at the military hospital today," Baba says, finger-combing his mustache.

Many years ago, before Mama and Baba were married, all men were given a choice—they could join the army for three years and fulfill their military obligation, or sign up as reservists and if there ever was a war, be called up for duty. Back then, Iraq was peaceful and thriving. Baba told us that people were happy and having a wonderful time.

He and Mama even went disco dancing. (We kids laugh and laugh at the thought of that!)

So Baba signed up for reservist duty. Soon after, the Iran war began and the reservists became active military. And my father, the dentist, became an army medic.

"Children!" My mother's voice interrupts my thoughts. "Get dressed. We're going to the central market."

"Mama," says Shireen, "we're already dressed." Shirzad, Ahmed, Shireen, and I had all slept in our clothes. Just in case we had to run of the house during the bombing and find a new place to stay.

Mama looks at us and blinks.

"Yes, of course," she says.

"Buy plenty," Baba tells her. "Who knows what the coming days will bring?" And he goes out the front door, off to his wartime work.

I should feel eager to follow him. After all, we have been cooped up in Shirzad's room all night.

But.

Again I wonder what it will look like outside. War could mean destruction. Death. I follow my family through the house and out the door.

"Nothing!" Ahmed says.

I look around the yard, at our house, and then up and down our street. Miraculously, everything looks the same.

"Nothing," Ahmed repeats. He sounds disappointed. I get it. For a younger kid, war can be exciting. I remember the thrill of finding a weapon shell casing or a crack in the street during the war with Iran.

But now that I'm older, I just feel very, very relieved.

"I can't believe it," I say to Shirzad.

"Good luck so far," my brother replies. "But who knows what the day will bring." He sounds like my father.

"Okay, Mister Glass Half Empty," I say. But as we all walk quickly toward the center of the city, I keep one eye on the sky. Just because it's daytime doesn't mean we're safe. The airplanes could come back at any time.

The market is a thirty-minute walk from our house. We want to get there early, before the food has been picked over. We're far from the only ones with this idea. As we walk, we are joined by others spilling out of their homes. The crowd grows as we near the market. We pick up our speed, trying to stay at the front of the crowd. Mama holds Shireen's hand, practically dragging her. We are silent, somber, on a mission.

Normally, a visit to the central market is a treat. Two miles across, filled with hundreds and hundreds of vendors' carts and trucks and tables loaded with food and other goods. In an area of the city that is mostly downtrodden and dusty, sand hued and sun parched, the market, with its chaos of colors and smells, has always been our oasis.

Butchers, bakers, farmers, grocers, and craftspeople. Spicy meats, fresh fruits and vegetables, sugary desserts and sweet candies! Fast food vendors selling shawarma wraps, kebabs, and falafel! Yogurt beverages and soda pops! The air filled with the smell of spices and smoke and the sounds of bargaining and arguing and laughter.

We reach the central market and . . . *what?*

"Where is everybody?" Shireen voices the question we're all thinking. Where are the vendors? Where are the trucks, the tables, the food? The only others we see are the ones who walked with us.

"Professor Abbas!" Mama calls out. A stout man pushes his way toward us.

"Sitt Khawlah!" He addresses Mama with her professional name. He must know Mama from her school.

"What is this?" Mama gestures around. "Where are the sellers—have you heard anything?"

The professor had. And what he'd heard was not good.

"The bridges have been destroyed," he says. "The farmers have no way to cross the river into the city. The Americans bombed the bridges to prevent the army from leaving the city."

"But it also prevents us from getting our food," Mama complains. "Once again, we are being made to suffer."

"By the evil Americans, of course," the professor says loudly.

"Of course," Mama says.

I know that the grownups don't really mean that. What they can't say out loud is the truth—that we are forced to suffer because of Saddam Hussein, not the Americans.

"I see a cart!" Shirzad is stretching to see above the crowd.

"Good luck to your family," Professor Abbas says hurriedly. He heads off in the direction where Shirzad is trying to see.

"Come, children," Mama says. "Before they sell out."

We join the frenzied circle of shoppers who surround the lone cart.

"Vegetables," Ahmed gripes bitterly. "Why couldn't it be chocolate?"

We leave the marketplace with near-empty arms and heavy hearts.

SIX

WE WALK HOME FROM THE MARKET. FEAR AND SHOCK and confusion swirl around us in the crowd.

"There's no more food!" an old lady wails. "We'll all starve!"

"If we have another night like last night they won't need to drop a bomb," a man says. "I'll be dead of a heart attack."

"Mama! Where's my mama?"

At the sound of a little girl's voice, Shireen's head swivels. She stops. My brothers and mother are pushing ahead.

"Keep moving," I tell my sister brusquely, and grab her hand.

"But she's lost," Shireen says. "Can't we help?"

No, I think. Rules of war told by parents, taught by teachers, learned from experience—don't stop, look straight ahead, numb your emotions, save yourself . . .

"I'm sure she'll be fine, Shireen," I say. "Let's play a guessing game. How many steps do you think it will take to get back to our street?"

We count our way toward home. By the time we have reached forty, the crowds have begun to thin and the road goes from one to two lanes. At one hundred, apartments turn into houses. The higher we count, the farther we get from downtown and the fancier things look.

"Two hundred seventy-three!" I announce as we turn the corner onto our street. Never very busy, today the road is eerily empty. No cars, no bicycles, no one out walking the dog.

Shireen and I catch up to the others at the entry gate to our yard.

"Mama," Shirzad is saying, "may we please stay outside? We'll be careful."

"Okay, okay." Mama waves us away. "Not you, Shireen. I need your help with lunch."

Ahmed is off like a shot into our backyard. He comes back carrying a ball.

If war is hell, then football is heaven.

During the previous war, the one against Iran, my parents gave up trying to keep three young boys cooped up inside.

"These boys are going to kill each other," Mama told our father then. "That is, if I don't kill them first."

Baba agreed with Mama. "All right," he said to us boys. "You may play outside, as long as you keep your eyes and ears open. Shirzad, you're in charge."

Shirzad puffed up with importance, but I didn't care. Anything to get out of the war-worried house.

When I wasn't playing outside during the last war, I could often be found bunkered under the back hall staircase, hiding from the Iranian infantry ground force. Some weeks, Iranian soldiers all over Basra. Other weeks, none. During breaks in the fighting we slept in our own beds, went to school, and played outside with our friends.

This war with America was obviously going to be different. First, I had grown too tall to fit under the stairs. Second, I now knew enough to realize that no staircase was going to protect me from a bomb.

And third, America and its allies were going to win.

In 1988, both Iraq and Iran claimed victory. (In reality, neither won. We all lost—family members, money, power, years of our lives . . .)

But this war against the world's biggest superpower? DUH, Saddam! Iraq is going to lose.

"Get ready to lose!" Ahmed shouts, kicking the black-and-white ball left foot to right foot to me.

I block the ball and pop it up. Dribbling from knee to knee, I scan the sky. No sign of aircraft. Or traffic. People are staying inside and saving their gas and oil for an emergency.

It gives us a nice, open football field. No sign of war.

I aim at an invisible goal beyond Shirzad's head and, kick! The ball flies past my brother.

"Go-o-o-o-o-o-al!" I yell, running around in mock celebration.

"Hey, guys!"

It's my best friend, Mustafa. He runs toward us, scooping up the ball on his way.

"Pass me the ball, Mustafa." Shirzad and Ahmed resume kicking the ball between them while I talk to my friend.

"I can't believe your grandmother let you out," I say. Mustafa's grandmother ruled their household and was notoriously overprotective.

"Mama convinced her." Mustafa grins. "She said 'new war, but same old Mustafa.'" Mustafa is hyperactive and clumsy—a combination that exasperates teachers at school and his family at home.

"Well, glad you made it out," I tell him, and we do our ritual hand slap.

"After last night, I'm just glad we're alive," Mustafa says. We talk for a minute about the crazy bombing and our even crazier good luck that it didn't affect our neighborhood.

Mustafa stops talking and frowns. I follow his gaze. Did he spot an aircraft? A soldier?

"Oh, brother," I groan. Actually, it's the brothers, plural. The twins, Omar and Umar. Omar jogs up and steals the ball from Ahmed. He kicks it up and starts dribbling it from one knee to the other.

Umar lumbers up and stands beside his twin. They aren't identical. But they are identically obnoxious. Omar is the mouth, Umar is the muscle.

"Three on three," Omar announces. "Me, Umar, and Mustafa against you Fadhils."

That isn't fair. Ahmed is so much younger, and the twins are strong players. Their team is clearly dominant. But my brothers and I don't argue.

We can't.

Omar and Umar are the sons of one of Saddam Hussein's top men. Anything we say or do could be reported to the twins' father. One false move, one ill-considered remark, and Saddam's henchmen will show up at our door.

They wouldn't bother with us kids. But my father would be taken away and then . . . Prison, torture, possibly even death.

This is serious. These twin meatheads have power, and they like to use it. A few weeks ago, a teacher punished Umar harshly for fighting. The teacher disappeared the next day. My mother told me that the teacher was "let go" and went to stay with relatives in Baghdad.

My mother is not a very good liar.

Anyway, the first rule of neighborhood football—keep your mouth shut and play.

Which we do. Using rocks as goal markers and the road as the field, we kick and pass and head the football back and forth. Our Fadhil team is down 1–0 (Umar is a brick wall of a goalie) when Ahmed kicks harder than I've ever seen him kick. The ball whizzes past Umar and just catches the inside corner by the stone.

"Goal!" Ahmed starts running in celebration.

Until Umar sticks his foot out and trips him. My little brother stumbles and falls.

Shirzad charges at Umar. The two throw a couple of punches. Umar gets Shirzad into a headlock and they grapple for a minute, but skinny Shirzad is no match for the brutish twin.

Just then, a shiny black sedan drives up our street. It stops next to Omar.

The passenger-side window goes down.

"Omarumar!" The twins' father shouts their names as if his sons were one person.

"Yes, sir!" Omar says. Umar releases Shirzad.

"Home! Now!" their father barks. His face is red and angry. I can see the mud brown of his uniform. The sight of a uniform from Saddam's Ba'ath Party makes me shudder.

"Yes, sir!" Both brothers take off running toward their home.

Suddenly I don't feel much like playing ball. Having one of Saddam's top men drive through our game is an unwelcome reminder of what—for a short time—we were able to forget.

War.

And it's only day two.

That evening, we all meet in Shirzad's bedroom, a.k.a the safe room. It feels less safe without my father, although I know that if he were here it wouldn't change a thing. Baba usually goes to work and comes back every night or two. Tonight, he is out there working and we are stuck here.

I block my ears when the first explosion erupts.

I send a mental message to the Americans: *Stay away from us.*

Then I lie on my mat and wait for whatever is to come.

SEVEN

FRIDAY, JANUARY 18, 1991 — DAY 3

Allahu Akbar, Allahu Akbar
(God is the greatest, God is the greatest)
Ashadu an la ilaha ill Allah
(I bear witness that there is none worthy of worship but
  God) . . .

I wake to the call for prayer. It streams through the neighborhood three times a day, every day, from a loud-speaker at the Shiite mosque.

Hayya'alas salah
(Come to prayer)
Hayya'alal falah
(Come to success)

Usually, I don't even notice the call. It fades into the

background noise of my life. But this morning, I lie on my mat half-awake and listen. We made it through another night. There was a lot less bombing nearby. The Americans must have been busy somewhere else.

La ilaha ill Allah
(There is no deity but God)

My family is not religious. We are Christian, but we don't go to church. I have friends who are Muslims and Christians and atheists.

I guess I don't believe in God, but what if I should? Which god should I pray to? Muhammed? Jesus Christ? Would it do me any good to pray for peace?

Allahu Akbar, Allahu Akbar . . .
La ilaha ill Allah . . .

And so another day begins.

Everyone gets up and goes to their room to get dressed. Mama and Shireen put breakfast on the table. Day-old bread and weak coffee.

Shirzad turns on the radio and takes Father's customary seat at the head of the table. It bugs me that he's considered the man of the family now, but I don't plan to listen to him. He's not my father.

The announcer is spouting off about "our great leader!" And how we are "destined for victory!"

No one says a word. My mother gets up and moves the dial, then sits back down. A different announcer is speaking. It's the Voice of America in Arabic. The Voice of America wants to reach non-English-speakers with a point of view that's different from what our state-run stations air.

"This is a new kind of war," says the announcer. "Gone are the days of newspaper reports hours—even days—later. Thanks to modern technology, this war has become a group event. Families, restaurant-goers, even college students gathering around the television. Not for a football game or a popular show, but for a war . . ."

"It's crazy," says Katie Putnam, a college student at New York University. "I thought we'd see soldiers and blood and stuff, but it looks, well, like a fireworks display."

The Voice of America resumes: "The bombing of Iraq is captured by nightvision video cameras. The missiles show up as glowing dots of light, arcing against a background of greenish Iraqi skies. Some have dubbed this 'the video game war,' because that's what it looks like."

My mother gets back up and snaps off the radio. She is frowning.

I meet my mother's eyes and shake my head as if to say *I can't believe it either.* A video game? Our damage and deaths and daily terror look like *a video game?*

Ugh.

I finish my breakfast and leave the table still hungry.

"Ali," Ahmed says. "Want to go treasure hunting?"

"Nah," I say. "Not today."

My brother frowns, then runs out of the room. He's going to scour the streets for spent shells or pieces of bombs.

I go to my room and lie on my bed. I woke up not long ago, but already I feel as weary as if I'd put in a full day.

I should be sort of happy. I mean, I could be going to school right now dressed in my school uniform—white shirt, dark blue or gray pants and a red cravat. Instead I'm in a gray T-shirt and jeans with a hole in the knee.

On a normal weekday, I'd be on my way to the middle school. My school is not in the best part of Basra. It's in the old city, which is crumbling and rough—more like an ancient city. I usually ride my bike to school, crossing the narrow part of the river on the pedestrian bridge that links our nice neighborhood and the ancestral town.

Our day at school starts at eight in the morning. We stand in group formations in the parking lot for ten minutes while the school principal conducts our daily quiz.

"What is the Ba'ath Party slogan?" the principal shouts.

In one voice our entire school replies: "Unity! Liberty! Socialism!"

Next the principal asks, "What are the Ba'ath Party's goals?"

Us: "One Arabic Nation with an Immortal Message!"

Then we march military style in a single line to our classrooms.

Classes begin. We stay in the same classroom while the teachers rotate in and out. Classes last 45 minutes. My favorite, of course, is English. History is okay, although it focuses on Iraqi history. I would like to learn a lot more about the rest of the world. Math? Ugh. Science—meh. Twice a week we have art class, where we draw themes of the Iraq-Iran war—Iraqi tanks, airplanes, soldiers killing the Iranian enemy. Art class might have been enjoyable if I had an ounce of artistic talent. I do not.

Physical education is nothing more than a PE teacher handing us a football and having us play in an open space outside.

I'm not a bad football player, but there are a few guys who are aggressive and prone to cheating behind the teacher's back. So my game focuses on staying out of their way.

Our school is all boys. Back in grade school, the boys and girls were in the same class together, although we stayed on opposite sides of the room and weren't supposed to talk to each other.

But middle school and high school are completely segregated. I miss glancing over at a cute girl. I wonder if the girls miss us? Probably not.

Anyway, earlier this winter, President Bush gave

Saddam's regime a January 15 deadline for withdrawing from Kuwait. In the weeks leading up to that day, no one could talk about anything but imminent war. Some kids said their families were leaving the city, going to stay with relatives who lived on farms.

At the final bell on January 14, though, we were uncharacteristically quiet. We said goodbye to each other, shaking hands or giving high-fives.

I wonder when—and if—school will start again.

I stay on my bed, my mind restless, my body not moving.

That night I toss and turn on my rug. The safe room feels anything but safe. My thoughts and heart race faster with every new sound I hear.

What was THAT? A bomb? How close? Am I going to die?

BOOM!

"Aaaugh!" I yell, bolting straight up.

In the dark I hear Ahmed and Shireen giggling.

"That was the bathroom door, dummy," says my sister. "Mom just went in."

"How was I supposed to know?" I grumble.

I do not like feeling so jumpy. There must be something I could do to stop feeling so . . . scared. I lie back down and shut my eyes. Behind my eyelids, an image appears.

A . . . bucket? Suddenly, I relax. I recognize that bucket. It's from my video game *Kaboom!* My hand instinctively curves around an imaginary paddle controller as I start to play.

Bombs begin dropping from the sky on the screen. Oh no! The mad bomber! I "move" my bucket back and forth, catching the bombs before they explode on the ground. My imaginary game play continues as I gain points and extra buckets while more and more bombs descend faster and faster. *Got it! Got it!* I rise up levels until . . . yes! I win! I WIN!

Somehow, fighting against an imaginary enemy calms me down. Take that, mad bomber! You can't kill me!

EIGHT

SUNDAY, JANUARY 20, 1991 — DAY 5

SADDAM SOUNDS TRIUMPHANT. AS WE SIT AT THE breakfast table, eating our bread with date jam, the radio blares out the news. Saddam's army has shot down and captured two American soldiers. They've been paraded around Baghdad and shown on American television. Saddam says they will be used as human shields.

"Today," Mama says, as she turns off the radio, "Shireen and I will clean the house, so you need to get out."

Shireen groans while we cheer. Shireen is often spoiled, but she is also the only female besides Mama, so she's stuck helping Mama cook and clean.

Ahmed races out of the house, with Shirzad and me jogging behind. Our day is spent exploring. Our neighborhood is basically intact; other places, not so much. Luckily we don't find any injured or dead people, but there's a lot of damage.

No houses are completely bombed, but some are missing chunks of walls.

"Run!" Ahmed shouts, so we all pick up the pace. We race, dodging obstacles like bricks and stones and rubble. We leap over pieces of metal that could be parts of bombs or cars or whatever. Jump! Dodge! Run! Around lunchtime Shirzad yells, "Race you home!" and we all muster up every bit of energy we have in hopes of being the one to finish first.

Lunch is rice. The regime has started rationing food. All Mama got from the store was coffee, lentils, cooking oil, and rice. I like rice, but as a *part* of a meal—not as a whole meal. Ugh.

"Thank goodness your father stocked up on wood," Mama says. "Although it is not going to last forever."

"The war won't last forever either," Ahmed observes, and shrugs. He looks around the table for someone to agree with him.

I don't want to think about how this war will play out. I mean, we're going to lose. But for how long will Saddam hold out? Maybe, hopefully, not too long. But probably he'll stay the stubborn leader he's always been and pretend everything is perfect!

While we get bombed to death.

You have to be patient in war. I learned that the last time, when we fought against Iran. It's not only about battles and bombs. There's a lot of just waiting.

Waiting in food lines. Waiting for leaders to make decisions. And *always*, waiting for the war to end.

When the war with Iran ended, I was eight. I'd imagined the scenario so many times, and I always pictured a big celebration with food and music and people cheering.

The reality was anticlimactic. The war ended *and nobody had won!* Our country and Iran agreed to a cease-fire. They announced it on TV—"The war has ended!" Mama went to wake up Baba, who was taking a nap between his hospital shift and leaving for work at his clinic.

We all watched together as the camera showed Saddam "making heroic decisions." Or that's what the broadcast said.

"Do you really think this is the end?" said Baba, shaking his head. "This is not the end. This man does not want peace."

Instead of holding a celebration in the streets, we were a nation of mourning. We had lost hundreds of thousands of our people. During the final thirty-six hours before the cease-fire, Saddam had sent waves and waves of soldiers into combat. So many died in a matter of hours.

There seemed to be no street or alley left without a mourning sign, a black piece of cloth with the name of the deceased in yellow and white. Some homes had more than one loss.

And on TV, they kept replaying our heroic leader "celebrating" our successes. Even a kid like me knew that this was horribly wrong.

Soon afterward, the massive reconstruction began. Over the next few months, foreigners—mostly from India—poured into our country to rebuild our roads and buildings with efficiency and expertise. And they worked what seemed like magic.

Basra was more beautiful and more modern than ever.

Until last April. When Saddam sent a hundred thousand troops into Kuwait, gouging black scars in the newly paved roads as armored tanks rolled through Basra en route to Kuwait City.

Baba was right. Saddam did not want peace. And though the world gave him plenty of chances to back out, to leave Kuwait alone, Saddam did not budge.

Leave it to our president to rebuild things only to have them ruined again.

Our roads. Our buildings.

Our spirits.

"The war won't last forever?" my little brother repeats. "Right?"

"Of course," my mother says. "Nothing lasts forever."

After lunch I go to my room and nap like a baby. Between the bombing at night and running around all morning, I'm exhausted.

While I sleep, I dream that I am the frog in the Frogger game. I'm hopping over animated bricks and stones and pieces of metal. Then the dream gets weird and I'm leaping over people's heads—Omar's and Umar's and Saddam's and celebrities' and grandparents'.

I wake up before I get splatted crossing the road of faces.

NINE

MONDAY, JANUARY 21, 1991 — DAY 6

FLIP. FLIP.

I'm lying on my bed, reading my Superman comics. I have over one hundred comics in my collection, my most prized possession.

Whenever the real world overwhelms me, I like to retreat into Superman's universe. I'm trying not to be depressed that I don't have a new comic to read. On a normal Monday after school I would stop at the corner market, where I would buy the newest issue. But a couple of weeks ago, the comics just stopped coming.

My comics are published in Arabic, but they have the same illustrations and stories as Superman comics around the world. Today I am immersed in an epic battle between Superman and Skyhook.

"Ali!" Shirzad bursts into my room without knocking.

"Get up. Mustafa is here. There's some crazy stuff going on at the high school."

"I'm busy," I say, dismissing him.

Whoomp! My brother lands on me. Hard.

My first instinct is to protect my comic. I hold it out, away from the knucklehead who is squashing me.

"All right, all right. Get off."

Shirzad rolls off me and watches as I carefully insert my comic in its rightful place. I keep my comics in numerical order on my bookcase.

"Let's go, freak," Shirzad says.

"Jealous," I counter. Shirzad wastes his allowance on candy and junk food.

With Superman in his proper place, I throw on a T-shirt and climb into my sneakers. We go out and meet Mustafa, who is hanging out on our front porch.

On American television, the girls are different from Basra girls. American girls wear T-shirts and jeans, just like boys. Basra girls wear dresses and skirts. American girls talk to boys and hang out casually with them. American teenagers date and hold hands and kiss.

In Basra, boys and girls basically stay apart. The only girls I've ever talked to much are my sister, Shireen, and my female cousins.

When we pass a small group of girls, I can't help it. I sneak a peek.

Usually, the girls do not notice me.

As the neighborhoods get increasingly downtrodden, Shirzad, Mustafa, and I begin jogging. People and buildings blur into one another as we pick up speed.

I reach the high school last, bemoaning my short legs. I feel even smaller when I see what's going on.

At least one hundred, maybe even two hundred high school guys dressed in youth military uniforms stand stiff and straight. They all hold long rifles called AK-47s against their shoulders, barrels pointed toward the sky.

One man stands apart, facing the squad. He barks orders, commands that I don't know but the squad does.

They spin their rifles, march in place, raise their arms, and shout, "Yes, sir!" At first, it looks so cool. And totally intimidating. I mean, it's like watching a high school football team in a championship game . . . with weapons. Any one of these guys would have intimidated me if I ran into him on the street.

And then, one guy stumbles. He bumps into the person next to him, who drops his gun. I tense, expecting the gun to go off, but fortunately the safety must be on.

The instructor goes nuts. Nuts! And then, in front of me, the military unity crumbles away. Guys start turning on each other. They shove, complain, or just walk away.

What was I thinking, being impressed by these guys?

The man in charge is no longer in charge. He has given up on yelling and walks over to us.

To my surprise, he slaps Mustafa on the back.

"Look at them," he says. "A bunch of clowns, right?"

"Ali Ahmed?" I say. "I didn't recognize you!"

Ali Ahmed is Mustafa's cousin. All the time he was growing up he came in and out of Mustafa's house, just as I did. When I was little, he used to throw me up on his shoulders and carry me around. When we played cowboys and Indians, he'd give me hints about where the enemy was and helped keep me in games longer than I would have if I'd been playing without him.

I look around at the armed soldiers. Most of them are teenagers, I realize now.

"Trust me," Ali Ahmed is saying, "this was not my first choice of assignments, but . . . You! Yes, you! Secure your rifle before you blow someone's head off! And the rest of you, get back in formation! Anyway, I'll do my part for the good of Iraq!"

Ali Ahmed salutes us but has one eyebrow raised, like he's not serious. He half hugs his cousin and marches back to his squad.

"Let's go," Shirzad says. We head home, barely talking. I have a weird feeling in my stomach, like something has been jarred loose.

The streets look different on our way back, as if we're viewing everything close up through a microscope.

I see a dusty walkway leading up to a crumbling brick apartment building. A small kid in just a T-shirt and no pants is banging a stick on a brick that has fallen — probably bombed — off his home.

I see an elderly woman in a head scarf, waving her arms wildly as she tells a story to a younger woman with wild frizzy hair who is leaning on a broom.

I pass a barefoot man with a bandaged head and a weeping woman with children standing nearby helplessly.

I see grimy, half-shattered windows and debris on the ground.

I don't smell food cooking. No spices, no sweetly baked treats, no coffee or steeping tea. The welcoming scents of the neighborhood are gone.

I feel weary and a bit sick. We walked all that way just to see teenagers with AK-47s. They were acting tough and brave, but really the brave people are the ones trying to stay safe and get though the day. These are my people.

We leave the older neighborhoods. Now there are yards filled with sand, many blocked off by stone walls. Others have iron fences. Through the black rails I see old men and young boys working together, with shovels and hand drills. Yard after yard, people are working on . . .

"Wells," Shirzad says, when Ahmed breaks the silence to ask. "The water companies have been bombed. The water pipes aren't flowing. Didn't you notice this morning?"

I'd noticed. Of course I'd noticed—the toilets not flushing, the rusty water coming out of our faucets. But, like the messes I left in my bedroom for the housecleaner to tidy, I'd stupidly assumed that someone else would take care of it.

"Yeah, I helped put together an outhouse yesterday," Mustafa says. "None of us knew what we were doing, so anyone can see in. Here's my street. See you tomorrow, if the bombs don't get you first."

"See you." I wave to my friend. I walk on with Shirzad, my hands in my pockets.

"Think we should dig a well?" I say.

"Or an outhouse," Shirzad responds.

"A well is easier," I point out. "It's just digging." I know neither of us has the skills or materials to build a structure.

At home, Shirzad and I recruit Ahmed to help. We find two good shovels in the back shed—one for Shirzad, one for me.

"What about me?" Ahmed whines.

"Here." Shirzad gives him a metal rake that we use sometimes to knock down ripe fruit from high branches.

"Cool!" says my little brother.

The three of us survey the backyard.

"Where do we start?" Ahmed asks.

"Near the old well," I say, sounding more sure of myself than I am. We find a circular iron cap that looks like it covers a well. We start digging a small distance away from it.

Three boys, two shovels, and a rake add up to nothing much.

Digging down less than a meter.

"We're almost to America!" Ahmed cheers, sticking the pole end of the rake in.

"Really, Ahmed?" Shirzad says. "What are you, four years old?"

"I was trying to stay positive." Ahmed makes a face at him, then throws his rake down and stomps off.

"This is an exercise in futility," I declare. "Even if we go farther who knows if we'll find water? We're in the desert."

"You're right. I know." My older brother wipes his brow. "I just feel like we need to do . . . something."

I nod. We put the tools back in the shed.

"Shirzad!" I say. "Remember what we did during the last war? The windows?"

"Right!" We race into the house. We look through cupboards and the pantry until—

"Jackpot!" Shirzad says. He holds up two rolls of heavy-duty tape. "And there's more back here. You know Mama and her stockpiling."

I grab a roll of tape from my brother. The two of us go to work taping the sides of the windows. The tape, hopefully, will hold the glass in the window frame, making it stronger and less likely to shatter.

"It looks safer," I say, admiring our finished work.

"I saw a couple bottles of Coke hidden in the back of the pantry," Shirzad says. "I think we've earned them."

I smile, probably for the first time today.

TEN

MY FATHER IS HOME! I'M OUTSIDE KICKING THE FOOT-
ball around when I see him coming up the street.

"Baba!" I shout, and I kick the ball up to my knees into
my hands. My father reaches me and puts his hand on my
head.

"Ali," he says, with a small smile. I look up at him. He
has dark, dark circles under his eyes. His usually carefully
trimmed mustache is sprouting hairs all which ways.

He tousles my hair and heads for the front door of the
house. I realize I can't remember the last time my father
touched me. We are not a family that readily shows affection
most of the time. My head still feels warm from my father's
hand.

I hear excited shrieks from inside. I go in the open front
door and see Shireen in my father's arms. Ahmed is jumping
up and down.

Mama comes out of the kitchen.

"Just in time for dinner," she says.

Shirzad bounds down the stairs, taking them two at a time. He and Baba high-five.

Our family is all together. Between the wars, this would have been normal and unappreciated. Now it seems like a holiday. I hope we have something special to eat.

Walking into the kitchen I see . . . bread and a bowl of date spread. *Oh, well.* Then my mother brings out some bottles of Coca-Cola.

That's more like it.

After washing up, Baba joins us at the table. We don't talk as we eat. The room feels peaceful.

Until Shirzad decides to open his mouth.

"How is the war going, Baba?" he asks.

My father puts his fork down. When he finishes chewing he says, "What?"

"I just wanted to know how things are going," Shirzad says. "You know, what you've seen, what you've heard."

Silence. Uh-oh. Shirzad has broken the unspoken rule. Don't ask about war.

"What I have seen and what I have heard are not conversation for the table," Baba says. "What I have seen and heard . . . you should be so blessed to never see or hear. In a few years you will be old enough to fight. Then you will know. Instead of Shirzad Fadhil you will be just another lamb sent out to the slaughter."

My father's voice has risen so he is almost yelling. During the last sentence he pounds the table with his fist, making the dishes jump.

"Baba, I'm sorry," Shirzad says. He looks like he is about to cry. "I just— I didn't know . . ."

"Good meal," Father says, and pushes back his chair. "I am going to rest."

We spend the afternoon quietly so as not to disturb Baba. At night we gather in the safe room. It feels safer with my father there. We fall asleep for a while.

"Mama! Papa!" Shireen cries out in the dark.

After what seems like forever, the outside goes quiet again. I don't hear the all clear siren, so it must be just a temporary lull.

Shireen whimpers in the dark.

"Shiri," Baba says. "Have I ever told you how I got your mama to marry me?"

Shireen shuts her whining. I can't help but smile. My little sister is obsessed with weddings. Her Barbies are always getting married.

"The story begins when I was finishing up dental school in Baghdad," Baba says.

Shireen isn't the only one listening. Baba is an excellent storyteller.

"It was selection day," continues Baba. "Where all the students learned where they would begin their practice."

"And you selected Basra!" Ahmed says.

"No, we were not allowed to choose what we wanted," Papa says. "Remember, all medical professionals, including dentists, work for the government. So the government had a system for assignments. We picked them out of a hat!"

We all laugh.

"I am serious." Baba's voice has a smile in it. "The names of towns and cities were written on slips of paper. I reached in and pulled out—"

He waits a moment as we lean in to hear more.

"Mosul!"

Mosul. That's all the way at the top of Iraq. Basra is at the bottom.

"Yes," Baba continues. "I thought, *All right, so it's Mosul for me.* But then my friend told me that his family lived in Mosul, and he was hoping to start his practice there. So I said, 'Let's switch.' We traded right there and then."

BOOM! Crack! Smash!

"Stay calm!" Baba shouts. "It's not our house! We're fine!"

Really, we're not fine. We are in a war, and we're being bombed. But no one argues the point.

After a few moments, the world outside resumes its quiet.

"Baba?" Shireen says, sounding very young and afraid. "Would you please finish the story?"

"Well," Baba says, "as you may have guessed, the new slip of paper in my palm said, 'Basra.'"

"It was your destiny!" Shireen gasps.

"It certainly wasn't the worst of the assignments," replies my father.

"And then you met Mama and lived happily ever . . ." My sister yawns and her voice trails off.

"Not exactly." My mother laughs. "But I think we'll save that part for another time."

Shireen fusses. I don't say anything, though I want to hear the rest of the story also. But my parents tell us to go to sleep.

As I'm drifting off, my mother's laugh echoes in my mind. I don't often hear her laugh. I replay that happy sound over and over in my head until I fall asleep.

ELEVEN

WEDNESDAY, JANUARY 23, 1991 — DAY 8

ANOTHER AFTERNOON OF FOOTBALL IN THE STREET. I used to live for the moments when the traffic was light enough to kick the ball around uninterrupted for a few minutes.

Now, thanks to the gas shortage, we have hours on our hands.

Kick! Pass! Stop! Goal!

"Go-o-o-o-al!" I shout, running around with my hands victoriously in the air.

"Plane!" Shirzad interrupts my celebration. He grabs my arm and drags me toward our house. We rush through the door in our privacy wall.

I stumble into my brother and we land hard on the dirt.

"Oof!" I roll onto my back and look up at the sky. The plane is flying high and is soon well past our neighborhood.

"Wadaeann," I say, and breathe a sigh of relief. *Goodbye.*

Shirzad nudges me in the side with his foot as he gets up off the ground.

"What, are you talking to your friends in the United States?" Shirzad teases. "Hey, Americans! Land here and pick up your buddy Ali Fadhil!"

"Oh, shut up," I tell him, but I'm smiling a little. It's no secret how I feel about the West.

Shirzad is standing, brushing himself off. He looks down at me with one eyebrow raised.

"Get real," he says. "We're Iraqi. You think they'd want you? That Saddam would ever let any of us out? Ha, ha, and ha."

"You'll see," I say. "I'll get there someday. And when I make my first million, I'll send for you in my private jet."

My brother snorts and shakes his head.

"Well, you wait out here to be rescued," he says. "I'm going in."

I don't say anything. I cross my arms behind my head and just lie there, staring at the sky.

Not a trace of the plane remains. Shirzad was joking, of course, but I can't help but let my mind wander back in time.

When I was very young, I thought that the way I lived was how everybody lived. I lived in a big house surrounded by sand. I had a nanny to take care of me and a housekeeper to clean up after me. I spoke Arabic, so everybody else must too, I thought. And then Baba brought home a TV for the family room. He and my mother had a small one in their bedroom, but *this* one, he said, was ours. Suddenly, we were allowed to watch shows—not only shows from Iraq but ones from America, too.

For the first time, I saw a world beyond my own. I saw forests and snow and the ocean. I saw people who looked different from people I had seen before. And I heard English. I don't remember why, but the English language—it, well, it *spoke* to me. My father and I learned to read the Arabic subtitles on the American shows and match them to some of the words. After watching cowboy Westerns, I'd yell, "Hands up!" and "Howdy, partner!" while playing with water pistols. I picked up TV catch phrases like "Pity the fool!" and "Book 'em, Danno," and repeated them endlessly without fully understanding what they meant.

When English classes began in fifth grade, I started getting my first A pluses. Translating Arabic, with its poetic, ancient words, to modern English was difficult for most of my classmates. But it came naturally to me. Now I could read, write, and speak English. I just didn't have anyone to speak it to.

"Hey, Americans!" I whisper to the sky. "I'm down here! It's me, Ali Fadhil!"

The sky is silent.

I close my eyes. If only I could trade places with an

American kid. I'd fit in, I know I would. I wear a T-shirt and jeans. I like sports and comic books. I speak English!

In the United States, I would see snow and forests and the ocean in reality, not just on TV, for the first time. I would say what I wanted to say without fear.

I would be safe. I would be free.

"Ali!" Shireen's voice pierces my fantasy. "Are you dead?"

I open my eyes. Shireen starts jumping over me. Back and forth.

"Okay, okay!" My little sister stops jumping. I hold out my hand as if I need help to get up.

Instead, I pull Shireen down with me and tickle her.

TWELVE

SADDAM'S TROOPS ARE BURNING THE KUWAITI OIL wells.

We heard it on the news. Typical Saddam Hussein. We invade Kuwait to take over their oil, and now we're wrecking it.

"Do you think this means we're losing already?" I ask Shirzad, dribbling the football a bit before kicking it to him.

"What?" Shirzad says, trapping the ball under his foot.

"Like he's saying, if I can't have this oil, then you can't either," I explain.

"Maybe." Shirzad kicks. "Or could be the fires will make the sky all smoky so the American pilots can't see."

"Oh yeah." I have to run left to stop the ball. *Kick!* "Do you think Baba is down there?" Baba told us that he and his medical team might move around from place to place, depending on where soldiers need medical treatment.

"Who knows?" my brother says. "Guess we'll have to wait until he comes off work to find out."

"Shirzad! Ali!" Mustafa jogs up the street toward us, followed by Omar and Umar and a few other boys from our neighborhood. "Let's play!"

I'm tired of trying to kick a ball past the cheating twins.

"Hide and seek!" I shout out.

"No, that's a baby game," sneers Umar.

"Then you don't have to play," I retort. I cover my eyes and start to count loudly. "*Wahid, ethnean, tlaatheh . . .*"

I hear no more complaints, just the sound of running. I count to twenty and then yell, "Ready or not, here I come!"

I look around, then head off toward the stone wall between our street and our house. As is my habit, I run my hands along the holes in the wall caused by bullets in the war with Iran before going through the entrance.

Our yard has great hiding places. It's a huge yard to match our huge house. I spot my first victim hiding behind the big eucalyptus tree. He takes off running to "safety," our front door, but I tag him easily. The twins are hiding around the right side of the house, inside the two-car garage.

"Do you two do everything the same?" I taunt, as I run around the garden tools and tag Omar. Umar manages to race out from behind my father's car and make a break for it.

"Tag, you're it!" I say to Omar. He ignores me and runs after his brother. "Cheater," I grumble.

I flush more guys out from behind orange trees and the tool shed next to the small garden. But they get away. That leaves Shirzad. I creep around the rest of the house without spotting him.

And then I see him. Walking up the pathway . . . with my father! I run up to give Baba a hug. But first I punch Shirzad in the arm.

"You're it!" I say.

After my father came home, he dusted himself off with dry towels and took a nap. Now, a couple of hours later, he has joined us for a lunch of tandoori bread and date spread.

"Okay, boys," he says, pushing away his empty plate. "Let's get to work."

Shirzad, Ahmed, and I follow Baba outside. Shireen brings up the rear until Mama grabs her and marches her back inside.

"Nice try," I hear Mama say over Shireen's protests.

My father takes out tools from the shed and a few things from the garage, and then he tells us what to do. An hour later, we've dug a well that spurts a small amount of water when you use a hand pump.

"Hurray!" Ahmed exclaims triumphantly.

"And now, we have one more project to do," Baba says. "Ali, you go get some empty bottles from the bottom bin in the pantry. Shirzad, I need the petrol cans from the garage

—even the one that's almost emptied out. Ahmed, go grab a few rags from the kitchen."

Finally! I feel like *finally* I am doing *something* to help my family.

But what exactly are we doing?

It turns out we are making a modified Molotov cocktail. But instead of using it as a flaming bomb, it will be used as a lamp.

"Very careful, boys," Baba warns. "This is not a toy." He shows us how to make the first one. Then we each make one, slowly pouring the gas into a bottle, wiping off the outside to make sure nothing spills . . . then a few more tweaks, and it's *done*.

Later that night, we black out our windows with dark sheets and light a Molotov lamp, its flame reaching no higher than the neck of the bottle—but still giving off light.

"Family game time!" Shireen cheers.

Baba taught us to play Monopoly. He knows English very well, so he translates the directions, even though we already know the colors of the properties and how to move our pieces around with the dice.

Place four Fadhil kids around a Monopoly game board and suddenly the mood gets Very. Serious. Shireen gets very competitive. Or I should say, Shireen with Baba backing her up.

We are immersed in the world of American paper dollar bills and tiny green houses when—

BOOM!!!

The nearby blast shakes our pieces all over the board and onto the floor.

"My houses!" Ahmed cries. "I almost had a hotel!"

It's true. My little brother is winning. *Was* winning.

"I lost the best blue property," Shirzad whines. "And I think my dog died."

I look behind me. The blast threw his little dog piece upside down on the floor. Other pieces and cards lay scattered around.

"Game. Over," I say in my best robotic video game voice.

THIRTEEN

"Sorry, kids," Baba says. "We need to save this."
He puts out the Molotov lamp.

Now it's pitch-black. I hear rumbling sounds from outside, but mostly it's quiet.

"And then what?" Shireen's voice pierces the night.

"What?" Baba and Mama say together.

"And then what happened after you moved to Basra, Baba?" Shireen asks. "How did you meet Mama?"

"I can tell you the rest of our story," Mama says. "As you know, I grew up here in Basra. I went to university in Baghdad for mathematics, then returned home to begin my teaching. One day, my father—your grandfather—had a bad toothache, and he asked me to take him to the new dentist nearby."

"Baba!" Shireen interjects.

"That's right. It was your father. He introduced himself

65

to me before fixing my father's tooth. I thought, what a polite dentist."

"Baba and I became friends," she says. "And then after some time, he went to my father and asked him for my hand in marriage."

I yawn. This story is putting me to sleep.

"Your grandfather said no," says Mama.

I wake up a little.

"So he went back and asked again to marry me," Mama says. "And again my father said no."

"Why?" Shireen and Ahmed both ask.

"Because Papa's Kurdish," Mama says. "My family was a respected Arab family. They did not want me to marry a Kurd."

My father *is* Kurdish.

"The Kurds are people with their own language and culture but without a nation to call their own," my fifth grade teacher said one day during a class on Iraq's history.

And that was *all* she said. Just one sentence to describe millions of people who live in the Middle East, many in our own country.

And then after school, some boys in my class taunted me. "Dirty Kurd! Stupid half-breed!"

"Ignorant jerks," I muttered, trying to dismiss them.

Until I got hit by a rock. I turned and charged one of

them, knocking him down. Another jumped on my back. We were in a three-person punch fest when we got pulled apart by a couple of lower-grade teachers.

"To the principal," one of them ordered.

"But . . . but that's not . . ." I was going to say "fair," but stopped when I saw the crowd of students that had formed to watch. The last thing I wanted was to sound like a whiner. A half-breed whiner.

I got three days' detention. After I explained the circumstances to my parents, they didn't punish me. My father was proud to be Kurdish. He was also quite aware that others looked down on his people.

Throughout history, Kurds, Christians, Jews, and Muslims have lived in Iraq. Sometimes different religions have gotten along, but not in my lifetime. In fact there are big problems *within* the religion of Islam.

There's one group called Sunni Muslims and another group called Shia Muslims. From what I can tell there's not much difference in their faith, but they disagree about who gets to lead the Muslim nation.

The Sunnis believe that the new caliph, or leader, should be elected from among those whose who are capable of the job. Shias believe that leaders should be directly related to the Prophet Muhammed. His descendants become leaders called imams.

Saddam Hussein is Sunni Muslim. He has ordered the deaths of Shia *and* Sunni Muslims—whoever gets in his way.

And he treats the Kurds the worst of all.

"So." Baba is still telling his tale. "It was not until the *third* try that I convinced your grandfather that I was worthy of marrying your mother. And so we became engaged, were married, and had the four of you."

"And you lived happily ever after!" says Shireen. Then my little sister adds, "Well, not exactly."

Even a six-year-old knows better than to believe a fairy tale during war.

What my little sister *doesn't* know is what happened to my father's people, the Kurds. Before I was born, my father's father—my jiddo—moved Baba's immediate family from northern Iraq down to Baghdad. They left their friends and family behind in the Kurdish region.

When I was nine, Saddam sent his cousin, General Ali Hassan al-Majid, to launch chemical attacks on the Iraqi Kurds. Chemical weapons. On his own people.

Saddam called the attacks "Anfal," the "spoils of war." That basically means, Go ahead, soldiers. Kill everyone and take their stuff afterward. The Anfal attacked and murdered one hundred and fifty thousand innocent people and injured thousands more.

Saddam rewarded his cousin, now known as Chemical

Ali, by making him governor of Kuwait. So the president of my country? Saddam Hussein. The governor of the newly invaded Kuwait? Chemical Ali.

"Stupid, stupid Saddam Hussein," I say under my breath, clenching my fists. I want to shout it, scream it at the top of my lungs. I want to yell curse words that carry through the airwaves all the way to Saddam's palace and drop like bombs on top of him.

FOURTEEN

"Up!" My mother's voice is sharp. "Boys! Shireen! Wake up!"

Five more minutes, I think while rolling over. I land on tile. I forgot I'm not in my bed. I really miss my bed.

"You need to go get our rations."

That gets us up. After twelve days of war, our food and drink supplies are pretty much gone. We now have to rely on government handouts.

And we need to get in line to do it. The earlier we reach the authorized ration supplier, a store in a strip mall, the better chance we have to get the full allotment of rations that are assigned to us.

"Ali and I will go, Mama," Shirzad says.

"What about me?" Ahmed whines.

"Ahmed," Shirzad says. "You stay here and be the man of the house while we're gone."

Baba has already left for work.

Ahmed takes the bait.

"You hear that, Shireen?" Ahmed boasts. Shireen looks up from her puzzle, spread out on the floor. She makes a sour face but nods.

Shirzad and I head to the front door.

"Good thinking about Ahmed," I say, tossing on my sneakers.

"I feel bad for the little guy," my brother says. *Huh.* I realize I do too. Before the war my little brother was always clowning around, pulling pranks. But now he is whiny and needy.

War has sucked the fun out of the little kids.

I shake off my thoughts, open the door, and stop.

"Do you smell that?" I ask Shirzad.

Shirzad shuts the door behind him and joins me on the front porch.

"Yes." He sniffs the air. "It smells like . . ." He thinks for a minute. It comes to him. "Baba's card games!"

"Right. Cigars," I say.

There is a light gray haze in the air. The scent sends my mind back to a memory of sitting on the stairs that lead to our basement, where my father and his friends held weekly card games.

"Come on," Shirzad says. "We need to get there fast."

We begin jogging down our street. A few streets later,

we pick up the pace. As I run, I jump over bricks. And crumbling stone. And things that might—or might not—be parts of bombs. I stop, lean over, and pick up a piece of twisted metal.

I feel like Pitfall Harry, the Atari character who runs through a mazelike jungle, jumping over pits and rolling logs and scorpions and crocodiles while grabbing treasures along the way. I am the war version of Pitfall Harry, dodging detritus and bomb parts.

I grab another piece of metal. This one has English letters and numbers on it!

"Yes!" I say. This is a real prize, something that can be traded for food or something else to help our family.

I am Harry again. I begin running, avoiding pitfalls. Hoping to make it to the end before time runs out. Shirzad runs too, to keep up with me.

And then we are there.

"Victory!" I exclaim, making a final leap and landing at the end of the line.

Shirzad looks at me sideways.

"We made it here in good time," I say quickly. No need to share my Pitfall Harry persona. Shirzad really doesn't have much of an imagination.

The ration line is pretty short, I think. Good news. There is hope we'll get our full share today.

Over the next few minutes, more and more people show up.

"I can't see the end of the line anymore," I say, casting a glance behind us.

The sun rises in the sky, shining a sickly grayish yellow light on account of the smog. The line does not move. To kill time, I entertain myself by translating other people's chatter into English. Well, I try to anyway.

Baby cries. No one sleeps. More spice. Not good taste. Face run hard.

All right. That last one does not translate so well.

Soldiers fire oil Kuwait City radio . . .

"Did you hear that?" I say in a low voice to Shirzad.

"Yes," says my brother, his face blank.

"What are you thinking?" I ask.

"Baba is supposed to be working in Kuwait City today," he answers.

The soldiers are setting fire to the oil wells in Kuwait City, a woman had said. I heard it on the radio.

"Baba will be okay," I say. "He won't be near the oil wells. He'll be with the medical unit."

"Right," says Shirzad. "But they have hundreds, maybe thousands of oil wells down there. That smoke we smell? It's got to be coming from there. If we can smell it half a mile away, it's got to be thick down there."

Oh. Saddam is destroying the oil because he can't have it. Typical Saddam. If he can't have what he wants, nobody can.

The city must seem like it's on fire.

"Baba will be okay," I repeat. But my voice isn't nearly as strong this time.

Shirzad just frowns.

"Finally!" An old woman shouts from the front of the line.

Shirzad and I step forward.

And then it's our turn.

"Fadhil," says Shirzad. "Fadhil."

The soldier in charge asks questions. "What is your address? How many in your household? Any infants?"

Another soldier listens to Shirzad's responses and dumps things into a cardboard box. He hands Shirzad the box.

"Next!" the soldier calls out.

"Thank you," my brother and I say, because we have to stay in the good graces of the ration police.

"Let me see what we've got," I say after we've moved a bit away. I'd recognized some of the items going in, but some were in bags or a smaller box that I couldn't see through.

"Not here," Shirzad says, holding the box away from my grasp.

"Just a look," I say. If there was one good thing, one treat even, Pitfall Harry's treasure would stack and ramp up the points in my "game."

A deep voice booms over the noise of the crowd.

"What are you doing? Where are you taking me? This is preposterous! I have done nothing wrong!"

Two Ba'athist soldiers are pulling a man out of the line.

"It's that professor!" I whisper to my brother. "Mother's friend from school!"

"Stay quiet!" Shirzad advises. "Ignore it."

But I can't help looking.

"Boy!" the professor suddenly shouts. "Teacher's son!"

I freeze. The professor's eyes are looking directly at me.

"Boy!" the professor calls. "Tell her . . . two *pi r!*"

One of the soldiers carrying the old man yanks a baton out of his belt and begins beating his captive. The professor flinches but does not cry out. His eyes are still locked on mine.

My head starts nodding, almost on its own. I nod and then very slowly form a thumbs-up, holding it for a moment before unclenching my fist and lowering my hand.

The professor smiles. The soldiers are handcuffing him and beating him, and he is smiling. As the soldiers drag him away, I see his hand. It is in a thumbs-up.

My mind is swirling. The professor is being taken away. When a person is taken away by Saddam's Ba'athist Party, he rarely comes back. And if he does, he's missing an arm or a tongue or his mind. Torture is just one tool in Saddam's toolbox.

FIFTEEN

"Do you want to see what's in this box or what?" Shirzad cuts into my thoughts.

"Yes," I say. I follow my brother to a spot far enough away from the line that people won't bother us or see what we got. It's none of their business if we happened to get something really good.

"Chickpeas, lentils, salt, coffee . . ." Shirzad peruses the contents.

I open the other box inside the bigger one to see what's inside.

"A shriveled eggplant, a loaf of bread that looks like a brick and feels like a brick."

"Good eating at the Fadhil table tonight," Shirzad says with a fake enthusiasm.

"Yum, yum." I rub my stomach, playing along.

"Shirzad! Hey!" A tall boy with a scraggly mustache jogs up to us.

"Yusef!" Shirzad grins. "Ali, I'm going to talk to Yusef for a couple minutes. I haven't seen this guy since the last day of school."

"Okay," I say. They walk away, Shirzad carefully guarding our rations box. *Now what am I supposed to do?*

"I'm going to start walking home!" I call to Shirzad's back. "You can catch up with me!"

I see the back of my brother's head nod. I start off in the direction of home.

I haven't gone far when I see the sun's glint bounce off a piece of shiny metal. I turn down a side street to see what it is. I jump over piles of stone to reach down and grab a nearly perfect rectangle of steel with the English "P-3" painted on it.

Pitfall Harry—back in the game! I think. When I'm done admiring the piece of metal, I look up to see three boys about my age. One of them has a large bandage over his eye.

"What have you got there?" says Eye Patch.

"Nothing," I say. "Junk."

I turn to walk away.

"Thief!" one of the boys says. I try to ignore him and keep walking, but then I hear shouts.

"Dirty Kurd!"

"Stinking Kurd thief!"

"Why don't you go back to where you came from?"

And . . . I turn back around, the hand not holding the metal scrap balling into a fist. Almost immediately, I realize that my reaction—to fight—is stupid. First, I'm not that great a fighter. Second, this is three against one.

"Hey," I say. I look closer at Eye Patch. "Kalif . . . Haram!" I try to keep my voice calm. I recognize the boys from my school.

"Is your eye okay?"

"Hand over the goods," Kalif says in a cold, hard voice. Kalif was in my class at school but we were in different sections. I don't know him really, and I don't remember him being mean. But war changes people.

"I'm leaving," I say. But when I turn to go, the boys move fast. They surround me.

"Give it. Now," Kalif growls. But I'm not about to hand it over.

I fake a move toward Kalif and then run between the two boys I don't know. It is one of my signature football moves, and it's much easier without dribbling a ball between my feet.

"Kurd!" Kalif shouts. "Ali!"

"Why are you boys out there staring at your navels?" a woman calls out from a window. "Get back in here and help me clean up this mess!"

"Yes, Mama," all three boys say in unison. I take a quick look back and instead of attackers, I see chastened sons. Another win for Pitfall Harry!

I start running again. Down an unfamiliar lane and onto another side street. I keep running in the direction I think will bring me around to the main road that leads home.

But the streets get narrower, more like lanes; the apartment buildings get older and dirtier, with garbage lying on the road. The buildings are closing in on me. I make my way down a narrow lane crowded with people. I push my way past old people and women in housedresses and head wraps. Little kids are everywhere.

All the people. The smell of garbage and smoke. The unfamiliar street. I start to feel dizzy, overwhelmed.

I stop and lean over, hands on my knees, panting heavily. Sweat trickles down the back of my neck. Around me, people have stopped too. They are staring at something. I slip between some tall people to take a look.

SIXTEEN

THERE ARE MEN IN THE STREET. I COUNT EIGHT OF them. Spread out in a line, facing my way. And then I see them. Three Ba'ath soldiers. With guns, pointed at the men in the street.

I realize what this is. It's a public execution.

No, no, NO! I whirl around to get out of there, when *Bam!* I hit a hard wall. I look up. It isn't a wall. It's a policeman. A very large Ba'athist policeman.

"Where do you think you're going?" he growls. He grabs the collar of my shirt and lifts me up so I'm forced to see him face to face.

"H-home?" I say.

He drops me and turns me around, still holding on to my shirt, then forces me through the crowd until we are right at the front. The eight men are still standing.

The three soldiers face them and raise their guns. Two of the men, wearing civilian clothes, drop to their knees.

"No!" I say, squirming to get away. But the policeman's hand stays clenched on my collar.

"Learn, boy," he says. "Tell your family. Tell your friends. This is what happens when you—"

Bang! The first man drops.

I flinch.

Bang! The next falls to the ground.

I turn my head. The policeman lets go of my collar and puts his hands on both sides of my head and twists it back so I have to watch.

Bang! A kneeling man falls forward.

Bang! The next guy . . . down.

Bang! Bang! Bang! Three more men go down in quick succession.

One is left standing. Not really a man; he looks more like a teenager. Standing alone, shaking.

Time seems to slow . . . down . . .

Bang! The young man cries out, "Oh!" and crumples to the ground. The red, blood-soaked ground.

"Remember," the policeman hisses in my ear. He drops his hold on my head.

I spin away and run, shoving my way past people,

running, running out of the crowd, away from the people, finally reaching a quiet street. I stumble over to a garbage can with no lid and vomit.

SEVENTEEN

I AM GASPING AND SPITTING WHEN I HEAR A GIRL'S voice.

"Are you sick? Do you need help? My name is Shirah."

I turn around, and wipe my mouth on my sleeve.

She is about Shireen's age, but with blond hair tied in a ponytail. She is barefoot.

"I'm all right," I tell her.

"Shirah! You know what Mama says! Don't talk to strangers!" an older girl yells, running up to us.

"His tummy is upset," the little girl says. "Are we supposed to just let him throw up on our street?"

She is feisty, like Shireen.

"I—" I say. "I used a can. N-not the street."

I stutter. Because I am talking to a girl.

In my country, girls are a foreign species.

"Can you tell me how to get to the new high school?" I

ask, glancing at the older girl. She has long blond hair like her sister, but she wears it loose down her back.

"There's no school anymore," the little girl, Shirah, says. "It was supposed to be my week to be teacher's helper. I waited for*ever* to be a helper."

"I know," I tell her. "I live near there. I'm trying to get home."

"It's not hard," says the older girl. She points and then gives me directions.

"Thank you," I say. "Thank you for your kindness."

"What's that in your hand?" asks Shirah.

"What?" I look down. I didn't realize. I'm still clutching the piece of steel.

"It's a treasure," I tell the little girl. "Here, you can have it."

"It's pretty!" Shirah says, taking it from my hand. "Look, Aisha, it's a bed for my doll!"

"You don't have to . . ." Aisha frowns a little, then relents. "All right, Shirah. But where are your manners? Tell the boy thank you."

"Thank you, boy," says Shirah, and she skips off.

"It's Ali," I say, more to Aisha than to Shirah, who is already too far away to hear.

Then I turn and run. And run, following Aisha's directions, until I make it to my neighborhood.

Pitfall Harry survives!

"I'm going to kill you!" My brother Shirzad's voice carries down our street. "Where were you? You were supposed to walk straight home."

I don't say a word. I am too out of breath.

"Ali! You stupid . . . I covered for you with Mama. I told everyone you were with Mustafa."

"Sorry," I pant. "I need water."

I head through the entry gate, Shirzad right behind me.

"That's it?" my brother demands. "Do you have any idea what it would have been like if anyone knew you went missing out there? Doesn't Mama have enough to worry about?"

A rush of memories flood my brain. The professor, the boys coming after me, the policeman and the eight men . . .

"I said I'm sorry!" I yell. "Now lay off! I'm fine. Everything's fine. Okay?"

Shirzad is quiet.

"Okay?" I repeat.

"Baba and his unit are missing," Shirzad says softly.

"What?" I say.

"Not officially," Shirzad amends.

"Mama's cousin Gilad is here. I overheard them talking in the kitchen when I was looking for you. Gilad is wounded and he just came back from the oil fields. He saw Baba's medical unit on his way in. On his way back, he went to the unit to get treatment, and they were gone. The area had been scorched."

"So what?" I counter. "They probably picked up and left."

"There were bodies," Shirzad says, so softly I can barely hear him.

"Boys!"

I jump. Mama opens the front door and sees us talking in the yard.

"Boys! Where are the rations?" she says. "You did get them, yes?"

"Yes, Mama," says Shirzad. "They are over there, under the tree in the shade."

"Well, bring them in," Mama says. "It's almost time for dinner. Cousin Gilad is here."

She shuts the door.

EIGHTEEN

"I WASN'T PLAYING AROUND," I PROTEST. "I GOT LOST."

"That's even more stupid!" Shirzad growls at me. "You can't even remember the way after *how* many times?"

I'm about to explain that a small mistake has turned into a horrifying one when the front door opens.

It's my cousin Gilad.

"Shirzad! Ali! Hello!" Gilad smiles. I don't say anything at first. Gilad doesn't look the way I remember him. First, he's in a soldier's uniform. Second, he's thin, almost gaunt, and he has a shaved head. Worse, there are stitches in places on his head. One ear looks like a chunk is missing . . . and one eye is covered with a white bandage.

"Hi!" my brother and I say.

The three of us go into the house and make our way to the kitchen.

"Finally!" Mama says. "Let me see what we've got here. It will be a special treat for our special guest."

"I'm not a guest, Ammah," says Gilad. "I'm family."

Shireen races into the kitchen and comes to an abrupt stop.

"Do you remember me?" Gilad says to her gently. "I'm your cousin Gilad."

Shireen puts a finger in her mouth and shakes her head.

"Last time I saw you we were at Grandma and Grandpa's, and you were much smaller," my cousin tells her. "And I had back then . . . Wait, I know." He bends down and says, "Camelback ride!"

Shireen takes her finger out of her mouth. "Cousin Camel Hump!" she shouts, and jumps on his back, wrapping her arms around his neck.

"You *do* remember!" Gilad says. "Because my name, Gilad, means camel's hump!"

"My name means sweet!" Shireen says. "Now, take me to the playroom, slave camel!" She strikes him with an imaginary whip.

"Gilad, maybe this is too much for you?" Mama says. "You should be resting . . ."

"Do not worry, Ammah." Gilad smiles. "Laughter is the best medicine."

Gilad marches off with Shireen shouting directions.

"Go on, boys," Mama says.

So Shirzad and I follow our cousin downstairs.

"Did you know," Gilad is saying, "that I used to carry Ali and Shirzad the same way when they were small?"

"Ali is still small," Shireen says. "Some of my friends are almost as tall as him."

Shirzad snorts. I feel my face turn red.

"I'm sure he'll grow to be really tall," Gilad says. "All right, mistress, the ride stops here."

Gilad eases her arms off his neck and lets her slide down his back.

"Look out for my hump!" he says.

I remember that. My cousin always said the same thing after giving us a ride.

Shireen runs ahead and climbs back up the stairs. Gilad, I notice, walks slowly, holding on to the railing. Shirzad and I exchange a look before following him.

Ahmed is in the playroom, lying on the floor surrounded by action figures.

"Don't mess with my setup," Ahmed tells Shireen.

My sister knows just the thing to say to annoy Ahmed.

"I wouldn't touch your dolls," she says, wrinkling her nose.

"They're not dolls!" Ahmed yells. "They're action figures! Oh . . ." His voice trails off when he sees Gilad.

"Cousin Camel Hump!" Ahmed's eyes go wide. "Cool!"

Gilad sits down on the floor, careful not to touch

Ahmed's action figures. While everyone stays to talk, I slip out of the room.

I go to my bedroom and lie down on my bed. I miss my bed. I am sick of sleeping in the safe room. I close my eyes. My mind is spinning. Visions of the day haunt me. Being called a dirty Kurd. The policeman. The shootings. The men dropping to the ground. The girls helping me. And Shirzad bossing me around. Feeling small and powerless. I'm too tired to cry. I open my eyes and they land on my favorite thing.

My comic book collection. There they are, neatly lined up in a box. I think about my favorite, an early Superman in which Clark Kent gets bullied and teased by his coworkers. And then he transforms into Superman and saves the city. I shut my eyes . . .

I'm inside the Superman video game. A bridge is out, one that connects the city to the rest of the civilized world. I'm in a Superman outfit and I'm flying over the city to the bridge. It is Lex Luthor, my nemesis, who has destroyed the bridge, but somehow his face is that of Saddam Hussein!

I fly around, capturing Saddam's minions and avoiding the kryptonite Saddam has released.

I succeed! I capture Saddam Hussein and put him in a prison. I race into the nearest phone booth and turn back into Clark Kent. Then I go back to my job at the Daily Planet, where Lois Lane is waiting for me. But Lois's face is that of the girl I just met on the street. The older sister. To win the game, Clark Kent must kiss Lois Lane.

I can't do it. I'm too scared and shy.

Game over.

"Ali! Wake up!" Shireen shakes my arm. "Time to eat."

I roll off the bed and stumble to the bathroom. I pee in the jar that stands in for a toilet during war. I leave it there for now and go downstairs.

NINETEEN

THE DINING ROOM TABLE IS SET AS IF WE WERE ABOUT
to have a fancy dinner. The good china plates and the shiny
silverware are laid out.

"You did not do this all for me?" Gilad frowns.

"Yes," Mama says, carrying a serving dish. She lays it on
the table. "Today we enjoy a meal with my sister's beloved
son."

I cannot believe it. On the platter is a feast. Eggplant,
rice, orange slices, and pita triangles! And—chocolate!"

"Mama—how?" Shirzad asks.

"I had a few things tucked away for a special day," says
Mama. "Sit. Eat."

We sit.

We eat.

The richness of the eggplant and rice, along with the
sweet orange and warm pita . . . it's indescribable. I chew

slowly to savor the flavors, and it seems that the next bite is even more delicious.

Finally, my stomach has something better to do than grumble and growl.

And then my food is all gone, except for the square of chocolate. I look around the table. Everyone has saved their chocolate for last, even the little kids.

Gilad picks his up and peels off the wrapper. Mama does the same. That does it. All four of us kids rip into our chocolates and . . . wow! *Sooooo good!*

Before the war we ate sweets all the time, and took them for granted. But today, one small piece of chocolate is heaven.

I see Mama give her square of chocolate to Shireen. Gilad gives his to Ahmed, who looks happier than I have seen him in a long time. With a smudge of chocolate on his face, he is actually smiling.

For a few more moments, the mood in the room feels light.

And then my cousin says something that changes things.

"Shirzad," he says. "You should be sitting here. It's your father's seat, right? You're the man of the family now."

Gilad gets up. He walks behind his chair and pulls it out, then gestures to it. My older brother, older by just one year, gets up and walks over. He stands in front of the chair, leans forward as he puts his hands under the seat, and pulls it forward as he sits down.

I look at Mama. She is sitting quietly.

"Wait!" I say. "That's Baba's seat."

"Baba isn't here," says Mama.

"But he will be!" My voice is rising. "Baba will be back."

"Sit down, Ali," Shirzad says, from his new place at the table.

"When is Baba coming back?" Shireen asks. "I miss him."

"We don't know," Mama says matter-of-factly. "But Gilad is right. Shirzad is the head of our house until Baba returns."

"Ali," Shirzad says again. "Sit down."

"Come on, Ali." Gilad walks over and puts his hand on my shoulder. "Sit back down. I have some good stories to tell."

I lower myself back into my seat. But I'm glaring at Shirzad. And when Gilad tells some funny stories about his dog and pet bird back home, I barely hear Ahmed's and Shireen's laughter.

Why did Gilad tell Shirzad to sit in Baba's seat? Does he know something about Baba that he's not telling us? If Baba is dead, why won't he tell us? This is war! People die!

"Is Baba dead?" I blurt out. Everyone turns to look at me. The laughing ends. "Is that why you came here, Gilad? To tell Mama that my father is dead? Is it?"

"Ali!" Mama says sharply. "Stop!"

"We deserve to know the truth," I insist.

"You're right, Ali," Gilad says. "The truth is . . . I really don't know. I was leaving Kuwait City on my way back to Baghdad and saw a portable medical unit that said BASRA on it. I got out of my friend's vehicle, walked over to it, and asked if they knew my uncle, and I was surprised to hear that this was his unit!"

"Really?" Ahmed says.

"Did you see my Baba?" asks Shireen.

"As I told your Mama, no." Gilad shakes his head. "I did not. He was busy out somewhere in the field. My buddy and I drove around looking for him. But it was too hard to see much through the smoke. So we went back to the Basra unit and . . . and . . . it had been shelled. Bullet holes were everywhere. Some people had been killed."

My mother covers her mouth, suppressing a small cry.

"Your father was not one of them," my cousin says hurriedly. "I did not see my uncle."

"You're sure?" I didn't realize I was holding my breath until I let it go.

"Yes," says Gilad. He stands up and holds out his hand to me, making clear that he is being honest. I shake it.

"Auntie," my cousin says. "Thank you for the wonderful meal. I have to be leaving."

"Already?" Mama frowns.

The call to prayer sounds from outside. Then a honk of a car horn.

"That's my ride." Gilad gives Mama a hug.

"How did you get a ride?" Shirzad asks.

I was thinking the same thing. There are so few cars on the road—only the highest-ranking people get gas rations.

"One advantage of growing up in Baghdad is that there are lots of Saddam's relatives around." Gilad grins. "I went to school with one of his nephews. Great guy, moved to Basra. He's taking me home."

Gilad gives us a mock salute and we follow him outside.

There's a black sedan with government license plates and a guy's head sticking out the window.

"Yo, Gilad!" he shouts in American English. "Let's rock and roll!"

Gilad gets in the car and waves. The car speeds away, leaving us standing on the front steps.

And then I feel a kick on my shin.

"You thought Baba was dead!" Shireen says to me. "You're so stupid!"

Everyone disperses—Mama and Shireen-the-shin-kicker to the kitchen to clean up, and Ahmed and Shirzad up the stairs.

I make my way across the floor, passing the stairs and the parlor and the guest bathroom.

I stand at the door of my father's study. I'm not allowed in there without permission. But Baba is not here. I take hold of the handle and push the door open. Shelves of books, piles of paper, framed pictures on the wall, and the faint scent of a cigar . . . It's as if nothing has changed in here. The room is the way it always was, waiting for my father to return at any moment. He's only been gone for a few days, but it feels like much longer.

I wander over to his desk, where a globe stands beside his pens and ashtray and paperweight.

I turn the globe to Iraq. My country is small compared to most. Will it exist after the world stops bombing us? Will it take the destruction of my country to get rid of Saddam?

I put my finger on tiny Basra and Baghdad and start to turn the globe again. I trace a path along the same latitude. Straight across . . . just above the 30 degrees latitude mark.

I land on Los Angeles, California, United States of America.

Huh, I think. We are on the same line as the movie stars. And all it took to get there was a quick spin of the globe. But that's just a fantasy. *Ha.*

In real life you don't go from Iraq to America. The closest I'll ever get to the United States is a finger on the globe, and I twirl it bitterly. As I leave my father's study, I can hear the world still spinning.

TWENTY

Tuesday, January 29, 1991 — Day 14

I'm lying on my bed reading my Superman comics. Since yesterday, I've spent a lot of time in here.

"Ali!" Shirzad bursts into my room without knocking.

He's the reason I've been stuck in my room. I'm hiding from him. I did not succeed.

"The garbage needs to go out," says my brother.

"So?" I grumble.

"Take it out now," he says. He holds out a small trash can.

I put down my comic and get off the bed.

"Yes, Dictator." I stand stick straight and salute him. "Sir," I say with a huff. Then I march stiffly past him and out the door.

I drag myself down the stairs. I'm not joking when I call Shirzad "Dictator." Our head of household is letting power go to his head.

Shirzad is right behind me.

"Then the bathrooms need cleaning," he says.

"What?" I stop at the bottom of the stairs and look up at him. "Bathrooms aren't my job, that's for—"

The housekeeper. Mama. Shireen. In the past, cleaning duties have gone to women.

"Make Shireen do it," I say.

"She's helping Mama all day," Shirzad says.

"Ahmed," I say.

"He's helping me tidy up the safe room and bring in wood," my brother counters.

"Well, I'm going out for a little while before I do it then," I tell him, and start walking.

"No," says Shirzad. "You're grounded."

I'm what? I stop dead in my tracks. That's something we see on American TV shows. The kid does something wrong and the parents ground him as a punishment.

"You can't be trusted to leave without getting lost," says Shirzad calmly.

But I am not calm. "You don't know anything! You can't make me! You're not the Saddam of our family!" I yell.

Then I punch Shirzad. I'm aiming for his face, but he moves and I get his shoulder.

I expect Shirzad to hit back. That's what we do. We fight until Mama or Baba breaks it up.

Shirzad doesn't hit back. Instead he says, "Grow up, Ali. Go take care of your responsibilities."

And he walks away.

That's it? Who does he think he is? I'm steaming mad as I go to the kitchen to get the trash container.

Mama is grinding a small mound of grain. The lack of decent food is starting to get to me. I'm hungry. But I don't complain. I just go do my darn chore.

Shireen walks into the kitchen.

"Mama, I'm hungry," she says. I look at my sister and shake my head no. Shireen is losing her baby fat. She looks older, less like "the baby."

"Mama," Shireen whines. "Mama, is Baba coming back today? I need him to fix my Barbie Dreamhouse elevator."

She still sounds like the baby.

"I don't know when Baba will be back," Mama tells Shireen for the millionth time. "And Barbie can walk up the stairs."

"I'm *hungry*," Shireen whimpers.

"Shireen," I say. "We're all hungry. Now leave Mama alone."

"Ali!" Mama says. "That was rude."

"Sorry," I tell Mama. "Sorry," I tell Shireen. My sister sticks her tongue out at me.

I look into the kitchen garbage pail. There's nothing in it but a few scraps of plastic wrapper. I add them to my pail.

"Ali," my mother says. "I need my glasses. I think I may have left them in my office."

"I'll get them," I say, putting down the trash.

My mother's office is small, with just a desk and a shelf filled mostly with math books.

Ugh . . . I think automatically. But then I see some small framed photos among the books.

There are class photos of each of us. There's a picture of my mother and father at their wedding and one of our family when Shireen was a baby.

Then I see one I hadn't really noticed before. There is my father with longish hair and a droopy mustache. My mother is wearing large dark sunglasses and her hair is loose. She is hugging a short, smiling woman. On the far right is a man who . . .

Wait a minute . . .

I look closer. I recognize this man. I saw him *yesterday* . . .

Before I saw my cousin Gilad . . .

Before I threw up in the street . . .

Before the eight men . . .

Before I got lost . . .

I was with Shirzad at the ration line and saw the professor get taken away.

I leave the papers on the desk and carry Mama's glasses to the kitchen.

"Mama," I say. "I saw Professor Abbas yesterday morning. He was being taken away by Saddam's men."

Mama stops what she was doing. She looks at me.

"He said to tell you something," I say. "Tell the math professor, he said."

"Shireen," says Mama. "Go find Shirzad and tell him to come here."

"Yes, Mama," Shireen says, without an argument. Something in Mama's voice means business.

I stand in awkward silence as my mother pounds and kneads a small mound of dough. She places it on a baking sheet and opens the oven.

"We will need more wood for the oven soon. Shirzad and Ahmed brought in the last of it this morning," Mama says quietly. "And there's still no gas."

"Yes, Mama," I reply. I don't know where to get wood. Papa always filled the wood pile. *Would Shirzad let me out to chop down a tree? Do we even have an ax?*

Shirzad comes into the kitchen with Shireen.

"Shiri," Mama says. "Go play in the playroom. I need to speak to Shirzad and Ali now."

Shireen runs out.

"Boys," Mama says, "this is very important. Tell me what happened with Professor Abbas."

We both talk over each other, but the main message is clear.

"He said the two pies are . . . something," I say.

". . . he was dragged away," Shirzad says.

"And then he gave me a thumbs-up," I add.

"I didn't see that." Shirzad looks at me.

"After I nodded that I'd tell Mama, he gave me a thumbs-up," I explain. "And I did it back." I make the gesture now.

"And he smiled," I say. "Mama, the professor smiled at me as they were taking him away."

Mama turns away, but not before I see a tear run down her cheek.

I look at Shirzad. He is stonefaced.

My mother takes a deep breath. Then she turns back and says, "What I'm about to tell you, you need to keep just between us, you understand?"

I nod.

"Let's go to the living room," she says.

Shirzad and I sit on the couch. Mama takes the recliner, where Baba relaxes and watches TV after work. The TV, of course, is off. I miss TV. I miss electricity.

"In the seventies," Mama says, "your father and I went disco dancing every Saturday night."

I can't help it. I laugh. *Disco?*

"Before you two were born," Mama continues, "things were very different. People were more open and lighthearted. Every week we would meet friends for dinner and dancing.

Afterward, we would stay out quite late, talking over coffee at a café."

Mama pauses and brushes some stray hairs behind her ear.

"Professor Abbas and his wife were among our group of friends, many of whom still teach at our school. We were all idealists back then, wanting to make Iraq a better place not only for ourselves and our families, but for everyone. The table at the café we sat around was a circle. So we nicknamed our group the Circle.

"Ali, you heard the professor say two *pi r*, which is a formula for the circumference of a circle, the measurement around a circle. He wanted me to let our friends around the Circle know he was taken away, when I am able to. When school starts again. He knew we would help take care of his wife and children.

"It is sad we have to speak in code." Mama sighs and closes her eyes. "We used to have such freedoms . . .

"Shirzad. Ali." Mama opens her eyes. "I want you to know that not long ago, things were different. Life was different. And I believe it can be that way again."

"Me too, Mama," Shirzad says.

I am silent with sadness.

TWENTY-ONE

THAT NIGHT, WHILE MY FAMILY SLEEPS AROUND ME IN the safe room, my mind races in all different directions.

Hate Saddam. Wish the Americans would kill him and get this all over with.

Baba has disappeared into smoke-choked air.

Those girls helped me a couple of days ago. There are good people out there.

Bang! Bang! Eight men dead.

A different life. Iraq wasn't always like this . . .

I have had a glimpse of a different life. It was just a few weeks ago, though it feels longer.

It was New Year's Eve. To celebrate the start of 1991, the governor of Iraq held a ball. A glamorous, extravagant party at the Governor's Mansion.

My family was there.

Baba is the governor's dentist. The governor, one of Saddam's top men, likes my father because he is smart and professional, and because he takes great care of the governor's teeth.

We were all invited to the ball.

I close my eyes and remember . . .

"Come on!" I urged Ahmed, who was still sitting in the back seat of the limousine.

Everyone else had gone through the gates already. I grabbed Ahmed's hand and pulled him out.

"I don't want to go!" my little brother moaned. "I hate this tie."

"We all hate wearing ties," I said. "But that's the price you pay for being a cool dude," I told him, making him smile.

Ahmed and I caught up with Shirzad and our parents. My father was carrying Shireen so she wouldn't dirty her ruffled white dress or white buckled shoes. My father was wearing a tuxedo, and Mama had on a sunset-colored ball gown.

We walked up the stone path that led to the front door. Two men in tuxedos, with assault rifles slung over their shoulders, greeted Mama and Baba and checked their names against the guest list.

"Welcome to the Governor's New Year's Ball," the man with the list said to each of us—even Shireen.

"Happy New Year!" my father replied, and we all passed through the arched doorway.

The room we entered was huge, with white marble floors and gold-patterned walls and a chandelier the size of a car hanging from the soaring high ceiling. While I was looking up at it, I stumbled into Shireen.

"Ow!" she said.

"Shh . . ." hissed Mama.

"Don't worry." A woman appeared and beckoned us to follow her.

"The ballroom is down this hallway to the right. But first . . . this is Miss Saeid. She'll take the children upstairs for their own party games."

"Up those stairs?" Shireen pointed to the white, shining marble staircase with a gold railing.

"Yes!" Miss Saeid exclaimed. "Come with me!" The name Saeid means happy in Arabic, and boy was this woman happy.

Baba put Shireen down, and she skipped over to the smiling woman.

"Go on." I nudged Ahmed, who rolled his eyes. But he joined Shireen.

"Did you see that Lamborghini behind us?" I said to Shirzad.

"Yes. I wonder who —" My brother was interrupted.

"Boys, you come too!" trilled Miss Happy.

"Go ahead, Ali, Shirzad," said Mama.

"We're not little kids," Shirzad protested.

"Are you under fourteen?" Miss Happy chirped.

Shirzad and I nodded.

"Then come with me!"

I took one last longing look at my parents. Then I walked with my brothers and sister up the fancy staircase.

We were taken to a room that could hold an entire soccer field. It was filled with kids—shrieking, running around, playing tag, making crafts, playing with toys. Ahmed and Shireen eagerly ran in and got lost amid the chaos. Miss Happy went in too.

Shirzad and I hung back in the hallway.

"Walk?" he said.

"Definitely," I responded. We explored the second floor. There were bedrooms—each one decorated differently. And almost as many bathrooms. Then we opened a door—

"—and it's an eight of spades! You're out, Hassan."

The boy dealing the deck of cards looked at us.

"Shirzad! Ali! How did they let you two in?"

It was Omar.

"Yeah, go get us some food," Umar said, chuckling. He stood against a wall with two other boys, all smoking hand-rolled cigarettes.

"We're guests," I said. "Just like you."

"Well, if you've got money, come join the game," said Omar.

"No, thank you," said Shirzad. "See you around."

My brother turned back into the hallway. I did too. We walked a little ways before I said, "No, thank you? Now you have to be all Mr. Manners with the twins?"

"Ali, their father is high up in the Ba'athist Party," Shirzad said. "Pretty much everyone here is, except for us and the servants. We need to be polite to everybody."

"I know. You're right." I saw a double door at the end of the corridor. We walked over to it and I pulled it open with two hands.

Sweet! It was a teenage boy's room. And a boy was in it. He had his hair cut military style and was wearing a suit and tie.

"Hi. You can call me Z," the boy said. "Want to play?"

Z? What kind of name is that?

He was playing on the latest game console.

"Yes!" Shirzad and I both said. We introduced ourselves. Shirzad flopped down on the second gamer chair. As Z switched over to two-player, I said, "Is this your room?"

"Yes," he said. "My father travels a lot and brings me books."

Then I saw it. A whole shelf of comics. Marvel, DC, Looney Tunes, and more. All organized, all in order.

"Great collection," I told Z. "Can I look at them?"

"Sure," he said.

I walked over and rifled through them. "You're missing number 17 and number 18 in Superman."

"Ali's obsessed with Superman," Shirzad said, playing video football.

"I was in New York City when those two comics came out," Z said. "I've been looking for them ever since."

"I've got them," I said, absently skimming the DC comics.

"You do?" Z paused the game.

"Yes. I have the full set."

"I'll pay you good money for those," said Z, looking straight at me.

"No way," I responded. "Those are my prized possessions."

"I respect that," Z said. "But the offer still stands."

He and Shirzad resumed their game play.

I watched as Z's team wiped out my brother's.

It was my turn to play, but before I got to, one of the twins showed up in the doorway.

"Z! Your father wants you downstairs . . ." Omar's voice trailed off when he saw us.

"I'll be right down," Z said.

"He said right now," Omar said. "Z, you know these guys?"

"Just met them. Their father cleans my teeth. Go on, O, I'll be right here."

Omar left. Z stood up slowly, as if he was in no hurry to comply with his father's request.

"Your father is a good dentist," he said loudly, as he walked to the door. He stuck his head out into the hallway and looked left, then right.

Then he came back into the room and said quietly, "Your father has your pictures in his office, That's how I knew who you are. Your father is a good man. Tell me, are you friends with Omar and Umar?"

"No," I said.

"They're our neighbors," Shirzad said, shooting me a warning look.

"I'd be careful around them," Z said. "They like to make trouble."

Z patted his hair down and turned back to the door.

"Play games as long as you like," he said. And he left us in his room.

I looked at Shirzad and shrugged. Well, all right. I sat down in the gamer chair that Z had occupied and started playing football.

"Z seems like a good guy," I said, maneuvering my players into position.

"His father is the governor," Shirzad said.

"I know," I replied as the game started.

"We need to keep our guard up," my brother said.

"I know that, too," I said. "I was just saying he's nice. I'm not going to say anything stupid."

My players were battling hard onscreen and Shirzad's were fighting hard too.

"Gooooooal!" my brother shouted.

Zero to one. Not for long.

We played all three periods and finished 4–4.

"Good game," Shirzad said. We stood and began to look around the room. I hadn't noticed that Z had his own mini fridge and microwave in one corner.

I had always thought we were born with a silver spoon in our mouth, but this kid was born with a golden spoon.

"Fooood!" some little kids screamed as they ran by in the hallway.

I was hungry, so I left the room and followed them down the hall and back downstairs to the main room.

Tables were set up with food and drinks. I grabbed a plate and filled it with delicious breads and cheeses and desserts.

I looked around to see where I could sit. A group of boys were off in a corner eating and laughing. I saw Omar and Umar and Z with other kids I didn't know.

What I did know was that I wouldn't be hanging out with them. They were Saddam's people. I was not.

I found Ahmed and Shireen and ate with them.

"Ten . . . nine . . . eight . . ."

It was the countdown to the new year.

"Seven . . . six . . . five . . ." The voices of the adults downstairs were so loud we could hear them, too. Shirzad joined us.

"Four . . . three . . ." I shouted along with my brothers and sister.

"Two . . . one . . . Happy New Year!"

It was 1991. I made a wish. Please let this be a really good year!

And then I joined the little kids who were playing tag, and I ran and laughed and enjoyed.

TWENTY-TWO

WEDNESDAY, JANUARY 30, 1991 — DAY 15,
TO FRIDAY, FEBRUARY 22, 1991 — DAY 38

EVERY DAY FEELS THE SAME LATELY.

Wake up to a gray haze that coats the morning sun.

Try to fill my l-o-n-g morning stuck around the house.

Eat a colorless lunch too small to fill my rumbling stomach.

Help clean the dust and ash off the floor and furniture.

Fall asleep from boredom.

Eat a bland dinner of grains and weak coffee.

Bunker down in the safe room as darkness falls over our city.

Hear bombs.

Be afraid.

Survive.

Repeat.

For two and a half weeks.

One night I can't sleep.

I imagine myself in a video game, Yar's Revenge. The objective is to destroy the evil Quotile, which exists on the other side of a barrier. My player, the Yar, must eat or shoot through the barrier in order to fire a cannon into the breach.

But the Quotile shoots at me with missiles so intense and fast that I must dodge and hide and retreat.

And when the Quotile turns into the Swirl, he is so dangerous and powerful that my Yar is no match for him.

Suddenly, the Swirl has Saddam's face, and I am moving and shooting and scoring points . . . but there seems to be no endgame. The Saddam Swirl is indestructible.

I wake up, covered in sweat. I am in Basra, not in a video game. It was just a nightmare.

I turn over to go to back to sleep.

Then I wake up in the morning to hear a fighter jet overhead.

My heart starts to race. What if he just dropped a bomb? What if more are coming? What if we are here one instant and gone the next?

Nothing happens.

I'm still alive, I think. Enough feeling sorry for myself, for being lazy.

I get up, step around my sleeping brother, and go to my own bedroom.

TWENTY-THREE

SATURDAY, FEBRUARY 23, 1991 — DAY 39

I LOOK AT MY ROW OF SUPERMAN COMICS. CLARK Kent is a regular guy until there's a problem . . . and then he becomes a superhero.

I wish I could talk to the American soldiers. Tell them to bomb Saddam's palaces — not us.

If I were Superman, I could fly to the planes and push them up to Baghdad and find Saddam and his henchmen and . . .

"Breakfast." Ahmed pokes his head in the door.

I go downstairs. In the kitchen, Mama gives me a plate of figs and cold lentils. And a cup of cold, weak coffee.

Mama sees the look on my face.

"We are all out of wood," she says. "I cannot heat the stove. Eat your food."

Ahmed and Shireen are already in the dining room.

"Where's Shirzad?" I ask.

"Out getting rations with his friends," Shireen says with her mouth full.

That does not improve my mood.

I sit down and shovel cold beans into my mouth.

"Mama!" I hear Shirzad slam the front door and run into the house. "Mama, turn on the radio!"

I quickly swallow some coffee to wash the taste of the beans out of my mouth. Then I run back upstairs to the safe room.

Shirzad is there, turning on the radio. We've barely been listening to it, because we're saving the batteries.

"What is it?" Mama rushes in.

A voice is announcing that the United States and its allies are preparing one of the largest land assaults in modern times. And that Saddam has declared that Iraq is ready to fight a ground war. Then the radio goes dead.

"Where are they going to fight?" I ask. "In Kuwait? Or Baghdad?"

"I don't know," Shirzad says. "Nobody knows exactly. But the largest land assault? That doesn't sound good."

"I don't want to get anyone's hopes up," Mama says. "But this could mean that the airplane bombing might slow down."

"But then their soldiers might be marching through," Shirad points out. "Going between Baghdad and Kuwait."

He's right. Basra lies directly on that route.

"I guess we'll know soon." Mama sighs, then goes over to the radio and lifts it up. "But not by radio. I'm afraid we've run out of batteries."

"Mama," I say, "may I please go out and look for Mustafa?"

My mother looks at Shirzad.

Grrrrrr . . . I think, as I keep a neutral face.

"Yes, Ali," my brother says. "But I'll need you later to help clean up the yard."

"Thanks," I say, and I take off before the Dictator changes his mind.

I race out the front door into the street.

Cough! Gag! Spit! The smoke in the air is so thick I can taste it.

I jog to Mustafa's house.

"Moooos!" I yell when I see him. He is bouncing a football on his knee.

"Ali!" my friend says. "You escaped."

"Shirzad is now the boss, and he is such a jerk!"

Mustafa laughs.

"Sorry, buddy," he says. "I saw him a couple days ago, and he told me you couldn't come out. He didn't say he was keeping you in, so I assumed you were in big trouble with your mother."

"I've been going crazy," I say. "Let's just play ball."

Mustafa knees the ball up in the air and kicks it straight to me.

I kick it back and it flies right over Mustafa's head.

"Sorry!" I cringe. "I'm out of practice."

We kick and pass and dribble and head the ball back and forth for a while.

"My father hasn't been home in a couple weeks," I say.

"Mine hasn't either," Mustafa responds.

Kick, stop.

"Think they're dead?" I ask.

"It's not looking good," my friend says. "What do you think?"

"I think they just can't get back," I say. "Maybe the roads aren't clear or they're being ordered to stay."

"I hope so," Mustafa says. His father is a businessman with a big smile and a big belly. Now he is a soldier, like most of the men.

We play some more, but I keep coughing and am out of breath.

"I'm done," I say. "This air is killing me." Then I add, "Not literally. My brother the tyrant wants me back to help him in the yard."

"You have to do chores?" Mustafa says. "We could be blown up any day. Who cares what your yard looks like?"

I shrug. "I know it."

"I'll walk back with you," my friend says. "But I'm not coming in. Shirzad might put me to work."

"You're lucky you're an only child," I grumble. I don't really mean it, but I'm still angry at Shirzad.

Mustafa leaves the ball in his yard.

"You guys got any food left?" he asks as we start heading toward my house.

"Barely," I say. "You?"

"Barely," he says.

Ugh. We used to talk about sports, vacations, and friends. Now we talk about starving.

"Hey, losers!"

"Perfect," I mutter. Omar and Umar are coming our way.

"Guess what?" says Omar.

"We're leaving!" says Umar.

Yes! I think.

"For good?" I say at the same time Mustafa says, "Where to?"

"It's classified." Omar smirks.

"We're going where it's safe," says Umar.

"Shut up," Omar tells his brother. "See you guys later. And good luck."

The twins pass by. When they're a good distance away, Mustafa says, "What did that mean?"

"They know something," I say, thinking of the land assault that I had just heard about on the radio.

We are close to my house. Shirzad is picking up branches and debris in our front yard.

"Ali!" Shirzad says. "I told you to come back and help."

"You didn't say when," I reply, sending a see-what-I-mean look to my friend. "And I'm here, aren't I? Hey, we just ran into the twins and they were acting weird."

"Weirder than usual," Mustafa says.

"Let me dump this stuff in the trash pile and then tell me about it," my brother says.

"You don't have to stay," I tell Mustafa.

"Trash pile," Mustafa muses. "I miss the garbage truck. I miss all trucks."

"And cars," I say. "And gas. And electricity. And sleeping in my own bed."

"And food," we say in unison. And sigh.

"And Coca-Cola," I say.

"Chocolate," says Mustafa.

TWENTY-FOUR

"SO WHAT'S UP WITH THE TWINS?" SHIRZAD IS BACK.

We tell him what they said.

"Somewhere safe?" Shirzad repeats. "So this street is unsafe?"

"That's what it sounded like to me," I say.

"I saw their father last night," Mustafa says. "He was driving to their house."

"Driving?" I ask.

"In his official Ba'athist car," Mustafa continues. "I was out walking and he practically ran me over."

"Omar had to come out with a flashlight and guide his dad into the driveway, it was so dark and smoky," says Mustafa.

The twins have a car, and they have gas for it, a flashlight and batteries, and now, some inside information? I hate them.

"Have you been out? I heard it was bad." Shirzad asks Mustafa.

"You mean outside this neighborhood?" Mustafa says. "Yes, everywhere has been hit. Some buildings are just . . . gone!"

"Why didn't you tell me this?" I turn to Shirzad. I feel like an idiot, feeling sorry for myself when at least I had a home in one piece.

Shirzad just says, "Sorry."

"Do you think it's because of Omar and Umar's father that nobody has bombed our street?" I ask. "So far, I mean?"

"That's definitely possible." Shirzad runs his hand through his hair. For the first time I notice how tired and old he looks. He's got a scraggly mustache and beard. My face is still smooth.

"But now they're gone," Mustafa says.

Unanswered questions hang in the air.

"Well," says Shirzad. "Gotta get back to the yard. Good seeing you, Mustafa. Come on, Ali."

"We're still cleaning the yard?" I can't believe this. "This might be our last day on earth and you want to spend it doing chores?"

"Uh, bye," says Mustafa hurriedly, and he ducks out before he gets stuck doing manual labor too.

"Or maybe Baba will come home and see that everything has been taken care of while he's away," says my brother.

"Or he's not coming home and this is a waste of time!" I yell.

"A waste of *your* time," Shirzad says. "I'm not going to stay out here to get shouted at. Make sure you clean around the shed. It's especially messy there."

I stand still as he goes inside. Then I pick up a rock and hurl it at the wall that separates our yard from the street. I pick up another one.

"This wall is your face, Shirzad," I say, and throw the rock hard at the wall.

"This wall is you, Saddam Hussein!" I pick up a larger, darker rock and pitch it like a fastball. It shatters against the wall into pieces and leaves a black mark behind.

"See?" I look up at the sky. "Now that's how you do it, Americans!"

I go to the shed and start cleaning up the yard.

Two hours later . . .

Done.

I put the broom and rake back into the shed. I carry the shriveled figs to the trash pile.

The yard looks as good as it can, considering there's a breeze that blows dust and smoke everywhere. I'm hot and dirty and tired. I wish I could take a shower, but we're stuck with wiping ourselves down with a rag.

I head into the house, careful to leave my shoes on the

steps outside. I'm so hungry; maybe Mama will let me grab a snack.

I walk into the kitchen.

"NO! Noooooooo!" I wail.

TWENTY-FIVE

MY MOTHER IS LIGHTING THE OVEN. SHE'S HOLDING a match to one of my Superman comics. It has caught, and the flame is eating away at the corners.

Mama doesn't look at me. She heats the oven and then tosses the comic into the sink and turns on the faucet.

"No . . ." I whisper, and run to the sink. I grab my comic. It's a charred, soggy mess!

Buried feelings burst out of me in an explosion of rage.

"How could you do this?" I scream at my mother. "It's not enough that everything has been hell for me, now you have to ruin the one good thing I have left?"

"I HATE YOU!" I shout with my whole being. I run toward my room, the mess of a comic dripping the whole way.

I kick open my bedroom door and slam it shut behind me. I frantically lay my comic out on the windowsill, hoping it will at least dry okay.

But not only are the corners burned off, the wet pages stick together.

Superman versus my mother. My mother is even stronger than kryptonite. This comic is ruined. It's not one of my top favorites, but it's a good one. Dead.

I can't help it. I burst into tears. I sink down onto the floor and bawl.

First, I cry about my precious Superman comic collection. Then everything catches up to me again. The horrors I've seen. The helplessness I feel. The hopelessness of war. My brother turning on me. My father. Baba.

I cry for a long, long time. I cry sitting on the floor. I get up and throw myself on the bed and sob until my throat feels raw and my tears have soaked my face and my blankets. I feel like I want to give up. I want to die. Finally I stop and take a deep, ragged breath.

There's a knock at the door.

I ignore it.

"Ali!" Shirzad calls. "Mama wants to talk to you."

I stay quiet, unmoving.

Shirzad goes away.

I close my eyes.

The Americans are coming. A ground war means soldiers will actually be on foot. They may even walk through Basra.

I open my eyes.

What if they come?

What if I see them?

Suddenly a slice of light penetrates my dark thoughts.

If I could talk to an American soldier, I could let him know that there's a kid who doesn't belong here. Sure, he might not be able to do anything immediately, but at least he'd *know*.

What if a whole troop comes through? I can make myself known to each one. *I could be seen and heard.*

I go to my school desk and pull open the drawer. If only my mother had looked in here, she would have found what she was looking for . . . plain paper. I tossed my notebook in here on the last day of school, along with a pencil. I open the notebook and flip past homework assignments until I find the unused pages near the back.

Now maybe I can be heard.

Coming up with the right message is not easy. Actually writing it? Even harder. Written Arabic goes right to left, with loops and dots and twirls. English goes left to right and has angles and straight lines and circles. So it takes more than a couple of pieces of precious paper before I get the words right.

My sign says: "I am Ali. I like American TV and I want to try pizza!"

I first wrote things like "Help! Take me with you!" And "Kill Saddam. Not us!"

But of course I had to rip up those pieces of paper. I cannot whisper those thoughts, let alone advertise them.

I carefully fold my sign in thirds the long way. Then I stick it in the back pocket of my jeans.

I leave my room and walk quickly and purposefully through the house and out the front door.

If Shirzad had given me a hard time, I would probably have punched him.

But nobody sees me.

I walk out of our yard and onto the street. I turn left and keep walking. I have no plan. I just keep walking. The odds of running into an American soldier are slim, but they aren't zero.

The streets are deserted. The hazy sky and smoky air keep most people inside. But soldiers have orders and in a ground war, they will be walking somewhere. Maybe here.

I walk through familiar streets and neighborhoods. Some streets have been bombed. Some houses are crumbled or damaged. Some look fine. But it's quiet out.

I walk in the eerily silent streets until I hear . . .

TWENTY-SIX

"Boy!"

An older woman in a black head wrap is sitting on the ground in her yard. I see a cane not too far from her.

I run over.

"Do you need help, ma'am?" I ask.

"Foolish me," the woman says. "I thought a walk would do me good. But, as you can see, I fell."

I take her arm and help her get up. I reach for her cane and hand it to her. I hold on to her until she seems steady.

"Would you please walk me inside?" she asks.

"Of course," I say.

I help her into her house and lead her to a chair. She sinks into it.

"Thank you, dear," the woman says. "My boys are soldiers, so I have been alone."

I see framed photos of two young men in uniform on the wall.

"I hope they come home safely," I say.

The woman is quiet for a moment. Then she says, "I want to thank you for your help. Is there something I can give you?"

"No, no," I say.

"I insist," she says.

I am about to ask for something to drink when another word pops out of my mouth.

"Batteries?" I ask. "Do you have any?"

"I do!" the woman says. "Go into my kitchen and look in the second drawer down."

I find a few batteries. Including two of the kind I need.

"This is great," I say. "I really appreciate it. Do you need anything else?"

"No, dear," the woman says.

"Well, thank you. I'm glad I could help."

I go to leave, but turn back.

"I'm Ali," I say.

"Nice to meet you, Ali," the woman says. "Your parents must be very proud of you."

My father is gone. My mother burned my comic book.

"Yes, ma'am," I say. I slip the batteries into my pocket and leave.

I set off for home.

I feel the paper in one pocket and the batteries in the other. I don't see anyone on my way back home.

When I'm almost there, I pull the paper out of my back pocket.

"I am Ali. I like American TV and I want to try pizza!"

What an idiot! What did I think—I'd meet some American soldier and he'd see how cool I am and would take me back with him to the United States?

I'm Iraqi. That's it. This is my life. No one is coming to help. I'm trapped here.

Forever.

I rip up the paper into little pieces and throw them on the ground. Then I stomp on them. *Dumb. Dumb. Dumb. I'm so dumb* . . .

And then I stop.

I look around. I'm an Iraqi, but I'm also half Kurdish. Kurds are fighters.

Fighters.

I have fighting blood in my veins. I may not be able to directly fight with my fists or a gun but I have . . . I have . . .

Heart.

I love my country. I love my family. I love life.

Anger drains out of my body as it is replaced by those thoughts.

I run to my house, fling open the door, and share the good news.

"I have batteries!"

TWENTY-SEVEN

WEDNESDAY, FEBRUARY 27, 1991 — DAY 43

"IT IS A VICTORY FOR OUR PEOPLE AND FOR PRESIDENT Saddam Hussein," a newscaster on Baghdad Radio is saying.

"We won?" Shireen asks, confused as usual.

"Shhh . . ." Mama shushes her and plays with the dial. It takes a little while to find a station that is telling the truth, not spewing propaganda.

"Iraq has accepted the cease-fire conditions imposed by America's President Bush," the voice says. "Iraqi troops will lay down their arms and pull out of Kuwait in full compliance with all United Nations Security Council resolutions.

"Six weeks since the start of Operation Desert Storm. Exactly one hundred hours since the ground war began. A temporary cease-fire is in effect."

My mother turns off the radio with a click that seems extra loud amid the silence.

"Does this mean I get my bedroom back?" Shirzad makes a weak joke.

"I think," Mama says slowly, "that we had better wait and see what happens. I hope this is the end, but war is not so predictable."

"Did we lose?" Shireen asks.

"Shireen," I say. "With Saddam as our leader, we always lose."

Mama says she has a headache and needs to lie down.

"Come on," Shirzad says. "Let's go outside and play tag."

"Even me?" says Shireen.

"Sure," my brother says. "You can be it first."

We go outside. I automatically look up and search the sky for bomber planes.

A temporary cease-fire, I think. No planes for now, if the cease-fire holds.

There is a slight breeze, which makes the smoky haze less of a problem. We play cautiously at first, giving our sister a chance to keep being it, but soon we are our full-out competitive selves.

"Tag! You're it!"

"No, you didn't get me!"

"Cheater!"

Shirzad grabs my shirt to tag me, and something inside me just snaps. Pent-up energy converts to sudden rage. I whirl around and punch him in the stomach. Next thing I know we're in a fist fight, pounding on each other.

I'm small but I'm quick. Shirzad has a longer reach and more strength. We're both landing some good blows and dodging others.

"You are *not* the boss of me!" I say, emphasizing my words with my fists.

"Yes. I. Am." Shirzad hits back.

"Dictator," I sneer.

"Idiot," he says. "Baby."

"I'm not a little kid," I say. "And *you're not my father!*"

I yell those last words at the top of my lungs.

Shirzad freezes. I misjudge my next move and punch air. I'm knocked off balance and fall to my knees.

"You're not my father," I repeat, but quietly. I look down. Drops of blood from my nose are forming a pattern on the ground. I hear my sister whimpering.

"I kept you safe, didn't I?" Shirzad yells. "Didn't I?"

I don't want to answer, to give in.

"Do you think I wanted this? I'd give anything for Baba to be back. I— I—" my brother's voice cracks. He lets loose a few curse words and runs away. I think I hear him crying as he goes.

I *am* an idiot, I realize. I've been thinking only of myself. It didn't occur to me that Shirzad might be hurting as much as I am.

I pull myself up to a standing position and pinch my nose to stop the bleeding.

"It's getting dark out," I tell Ahmed and Shireen. "Let's go inside."

"I'm telling Mama you boys were fighting," says Shireen.

"No, you aren't," Ahmed says. "If you tattle, there'll be trouble. Get it?"

Shireen rolls her eyes but doesn't say anything.

I head inside. I go straight to my room. My nose has stopped bleeding, and my physical pain has lessened. But a new pain stabs my heart. I see my collection of comics.

They are listing a bit to the right, instead of standing straight between the bookends. Three comics. My mother took three from the middle of the series.

They are not my top favorites, but they're not my least favorites either.

I had enjoyed collecting them, individually, but more important, as a full set. My *collection*. Now incomplete.

"Ali!" Shireen knocks on my door. "Dinner is ready!"

Who cares? I think.

"ALI!" Shireen's big mouth screeches.

"I'm not hungry!" I yell back. That, of course, is a lie. Of course I'm hungry. We're all hungry. But I can't face my mother yet. I'm still too angry.

"Aaaugh!" I kick my bookcase in frustration. "Owwwww!" *My toe!*

My comics wobble, but they stay in place. Only one book falls out — my English language workbook.

I lean over, pick it up, and hobble over to my bed. I lie down, foot throbbing.

Intermediate English. My workbook is only half done, since school has been canceled. I get up and grab a pencil and fall back onto my bed.

Prepositions:

1. at
2. after
3. around
4. before

I begin filling in the blanks on Practice Questions #1–#15.

1. I look (at) my comics.
2. (After) my mother burned my comics, I was mad.
3. I walk (around) my room.
4. (Before) today, I had a full set of comics.

I continue writing English sentences. I'm up to #12 . . . when there is a soft knock (on) (#10) my door.

TWENTY-EIGHT

"WHAT?" I SAY.

The door opens.

"It's me," says Mama. "I bring a peace offering."

She comes over and sets a plate down on my bedside table.

"Is that . . . ?" My eyes bug out.

"Lavash," Mama nods. "With tahini!"

I can't believe it—on my plate are two large pieces of flatbread slathered with tahini spread—a creamy butter made from crushed sesame seeds!

"Wha—? H-how?" I sputter.

"The governor's wife sent her maid over with the ingredients this morning," says Mama. "She also sent this note."

My mother hands me a fancy card embellished with a gold monogram of the governor's initials.

Dear Um Shirzad,

It was lovely talking with you on New Year's Eve.
Thank you to your family for attending our celebration!
I hope to meet again when circumstances permit.

I was thinking about your charming children and
thought they might enjoy these special treats. My son
sends his best wishes to your two eldest.

Sincerely,

Um Qusay

I look up at my mother.

"I spent some time talking with the governor's wife about her concerns about her children's education," Mama said. "And gave her some advice. She was very kind. And evidently, you and Shirzad made an impression on one of her sons."

The kid who shared his video games! I knew he was cool!

"Wow," I say, with my mouth full. I couldn't help but dig into the food before my mother stopped talking.

"I'll let you eat," said Mama. "But first, I want to apologize. I did not realize how important those comic books were to you. I knew you had read them, so I assumed you were finished with them."

I swallow and look down.

"How could you not know," I say quietly, "about my favorite thing in the world?"

"Ali." Mama sighs. "It is not easy being a working mother. Sometimes I was so busy paying attention to other people's children that I lost track of my own."

I don't know what to say.

"I thought cartoon paper would be easiest to burn," she adds. "I guess I should have used your math book instead."

I look up. Mama's mouth is serious, but her eyes are twinkling.

My mother joking about math?

I can't help it. I smile.

"Now enjoy your dinner," Mama says, and she leaves my room and shuts the door behind her.

Mmmmm. Yummm. The tahini melts perfectly into the warm bread . . . wait!

I sit up. *Warm* bread? I am a dummy. My mother ran out of gas and wood to light the oven. We were all so hungry. And then a gift of food shows up at the door.

I see it from my mother's perspective. The chance to feed her children good hot food versus a few highly flammable comics.

I look over at my comic collection. I'm sad about it.

With a mouthful of delicious food, I pick up my plate and my bottle of Coke. I go downstairs. Everyone is still in the dining room, looking happier and more relaxed than I've seen them look in a long time.

The conversation stops as I walk in the room.

"I-I . . ." I say. "I think that Superman saved the day!"

It's good to hear everyone laugh. I join in.

I open the Coke and hear the satisfying hiss of carbonation.

I relish every sip and every bite.

TWENTY-NINE

THURSDAY, FEBRUARY 28, 1991 — DAY 44

"WAKE UP!" WORDS ARE INVADING MY EAR AND POKing at my sleep.

"Ali! Wake up!" It's Shirzad.

"What?" I say, eyes closed.

"Shhh . . . get up! You have to see this!" My brother yanks off my blanket.

I open my eyes. I see Shirzad's feet. I'm sleeping on the blanketed floor of the safe room with the rest of the family. We still don't know if we are really safe. The war has not been officially announced as over. I follow Shirzad to my room, which overlooks the front yard. Down on the street is a man. A soldier in Ba'athist uniform. He is walking past our house, not in the brisk soldier way but slowly.

"And over there." Shirzad points.

Two soldiers. Down the street. It looks like one is leaning on the other.

"They were just in front of here," my brother says. "It looks like one injured his leg and the other is carrying him along."

"Who are they?" I ask. "Where are they going? And wait . . . they don't have any guns."

What good are soldiers without weapons?

"I'm going to go find out," Shirzad says, and races out of the room. I take off right behind him.

I run down the stairs and gain ground on Shirzad. Before he can open the front door, I'm standing in front of it.

"I'm going out with you," I say. And then, although the word almost sticks in my mouth, I add: "Please."

"Come on," my brother says. I step away to let him unlock and open the door. We both race outside, into the street and up to one of the soldiers.

"Excuse me," Shirzad says. "Sir."

The soldier stops. He stares blankly at us.

"We were just, uh, wondering . . ." Shirad falters.

"Where are you coming from?" I ask. "Where are you going?"

"I'm coming from hell," the soldier says. "I'm going home."

He starts walking away from us. When he's out of hearing range, I say, "That was creepy."

"I think he's shell-shocked," Shirzad says. "Not right in the head. Hey! There's more!"

A new pair of soldiers is on our street. We run up to them.

I ask the same questions. "Where are you coming from? Where are you going?"

"Got a cigarette?" one soldier asks.

"No, sorry," Shirzad responds.

"We're coming from Kuwait City," the other soldier says. "We were in our tank, part of a convoy, moving north along Route 80 when the enemy planes showed up and bombed us to pieces."

Route 80. Also known as the Basra-Kuwait Highway.

"It was crazy, man," says the soldier who asked for a cigarette. "We had to walk miles, and everywhere we saw burned vehicles and burned bodies . . ."

"These are just kids," the other guy reminds him, referring to us.

"And the smell of the oil wells and the charred corpses and burning gas . . . it was a highway of death. Yes, a highway of death."

"We're lucky to be alive," the other soldier says. "We just want to get home. We're a little lost. Which way to Baghdad?"

Shirzad gives him basic directions to a route that leads to Baghdad.

We wish the men luck.

Then we run into the house to find Mama.

Over weak coffee, we tell her what the soldiers said.

"They're coming home," my mother says. "Our soldiers are leaving Kuwait and coming back. This means they're in retreat. The war is really coming to an end."

"Baba may get back today," says Shirzad. "Those men made it. Baba could too."

We sit in a silence heavy with hope and fear.

"It's going to be hard to sit around and wait," admits Mama. "Let's keep the younger two busy. We could do chores . . . or play a game."

"Game!" my brother and I shout quickly.

And no game lasts longer than Monopoly.

By the time Ahmed and Shireen wake up, the Monopoly board has been set up, the money has been sorted, the cards are in place, and we're ready for Go.

Even Mama joins us in the playroom. The game gets competitive fast.

"Boardwalk!" Ahmed yells. He purchases it and eyes my properties. I own Park Place.

"No trade," I tell him. It's my turn. I roll the dice. I move my piece and land on Community Chest. I take a card.

"You have won second place in a beauty contest," I read. "Collect ten dollars."

My brothers jeer at me.

"I won first place," Shireen says.

"Okay, okay, just give me my money," I say to Shirzad, the banker.

It's Mama's turn.

"Free parking!" she says, scooping up the money in the middle.

The rest of us groan.

Ahmed picks up the dice and shakes them. Just as he's about to toss them . . .

"Who's winning?" A voice comes from the doorway.

"Baba!" Shireen shrieks and jumps up, knocking the board into disarray. Ahmed drops the dice.

My father is home! He's alive!

THIRTY

WE RUN OVER TO HIM, TRIPPING OVER ONE ANOTHER to hug him.

"Baba, where were you?"

"Are you all right?"

"Come get a cup of coffee and something to eat."

That last statement is from my mother.

We disentangle from Baba and walk downstairs with him. Mama tells us to set the table—the *head* of the table —with the good china and silverware.

When we sit down, I let out a big sigh. What a relief to have Shirzad at his regular place—a *kid's* seat, and my father as the rightful head of the family.

"Lavash!" My father says. "And Coca-Cola? What a wonderful welcome home!"

Mama tells him about the governor's wife while he eats. I watch him. He looks thin and tired. He is covered in soot.

But I don't see any injuries. After he swallows his last gulp of Coke, he burps. I can't help but giggle, mostly out of pure release of tension.

"Excuse me," Baba says, smiling.

"I'll try to tell you everything," he says. "But first, I am fine. I was moved to a hospital, where I was forced to stay and treat the injured. But it worked out well for me, because the hospital was on the outskirts of Kuwait City, not so close to the oil wells or the main fighting."

"And you made it!" says Ahmed.

I look at my younger brother. I see some of that spark coming back into his eyes. Shireen can't stop bouncing around with excitement. And my mother is looking at my father with affection.

I shoot a look at Shirzad. He grins at me. I know it's childish, but I stick my tongue out at him. *Ha, ha, you're not my boss anymore.* He replies with a rude hand gesture.

Yes. Things are getting back to normal.

"Kids," Baba says, "what I am about to tell you, before we go anywhere or do anything else, is very important."

"Should we . . ." Mama motions toward Shireen.

"She needs to hear this too," Baba says. He pats his knee and Shireen runs over and climbs up on his lap. My father strokes her hair as he talks.

"First, I am profoundly grateful that each of you is safe. The joy I felt walking up the stairs and hearing you playing

Monopoly . . ." Baba wipes his eyes. "It made my heart soar. Thank you for your hard work and patience and sacrifice. I came home to a house and a family that were well taken care of." He stops and looks at Shirzad.

"Shirzad, you have made me proud. You all make me proud."

My father smiles at each of us.

"And I know that you'll continue to make me proud, as our country and our friends move forward into the next chapter of our lives."

Wow. I admit it. This speech makes me sit up straighter. And maybe that's a tear in my eye . . . I wipe it away before anyone can see.

"However, first we need to close this chapter." My father frowns. "Just because the war is ending, it doesn't mean our troubles are. I've been hearing that most of the electricity and energy plants have been destroyed. Our roads and bridges have been bombed out. We can't communicate with our friends and family in other cities. And it may be a while before we'll be eating good food again on a regular basis.

"But we will get through this. We are strong. And we are together."

"The war is over!" shouts Ahmed. "Hurray!"

"Finally!" says Shireen. "It went on *forever!*"

Shirzad and I crack up. The war with Iran lasted eight years. This one was only about forty *days.*

"I was fortunate enough to be part of one of the first groups of people to make it back from Kuwait," my father says.

"Did you come up on Highway 80?" I ask. I almost say "the highway of death" but catch myself in time.

My father looks at me sadly.

"Yes," he says. "And there are many, many men behind me, now that Saddam has ordered the army to pull out of Kuwait. The Basra-Kuwait Highway is the only route back, so nearly everyone will be passing through or around Basra on their way home. I will be busy treating injuries and helping our soldiers. But for right now, I'm going to take a nap. So, no loud noises."

"Yes!" screams Ahmed. Shireen punches him in the shoulder.

"He said no noise!" she yells at Ahmed. The two of them start to bicker.

Everything is getting back to normal, I think to myself. *Or at least the new normal. Whatever that will be.*

THIRTY-ONE

WE ARE BACK IN SHIRZAD'S ROOM, FORMERLY THE safe room. But this time, we are not hiding. We are moving out. Everyone can sleep in their own room tonight.

"You're doing it wrong, Ahmed!" Shireen is getting back to her bossy self rather quickly.

"Then you do it yourself," Ahmed says, and he drops the corner of the rug he was rolling up. Ahmed runs and jumps on Shirzad's back. "Attack!"

Shirzad spins Ahmed around a couple times and dumps him onto the bed.

"Counterattack!" my older brother says, and pins Ahmed down for a few seconds before letting him up.

"Boys," Mama says, "enough." But she has a small smile on her lips.

I finish rolling up my rug and tuck it under my arm. I'm ready to take it out of here for good.

"President Hussein is triumphant!" a voice booms out from the radio.

I stop.

"Our fearless leader has stood up to George Bush and America, and stands today strong and determined, the father of his people . . ."

"Enough," says Baba, and turns the radio off.

"We lost, didn't we?" Shireen says. "We lost the war."

"Yes, Shireen," says Baba. "Iraq lost the war. But we are still here."

And so is Saddam.

Even the Americans couldn't get rid of Saddam.

What was it all for? I wonder. Forty-two days. Of battling, of bombing, of fear and hunger! And for so many families, grief and mourning. And the one man who set all this in motion is still going to be our leader, with all his palaces and luxuries and power.

What was this all for?

I shake my head and carry my rug to the playroom, where it will be stored in the closet, for a long time I hope. As I walk across the playroom, I trip over something. It's the cord that connects the joystick to the Atari console.

I don't fall; I just stumble a little.

Was it really just forty-two days ago that Shirzad and I sat in here playing video games?

I kick the controller closer to the entertainment center

that holds the TV. There will be no TV or video games until the electricity comes back, and who knows how long that will take?

I clench my hands into fists. My fingers are itching to grasp a controller and press the buttons and play a game. *I just want to play Atari!*

Instead I stand in the middle of the room, staring at a blank TV.

What do I do now? It's a strange feeling, having nothing to do. I've been in survival mode . . . How do I get back to living?

"Ali!" Ahmed bursts in carrying a football.

"Yes, Ahmed," I say, halfheartedly.

"Come on," Ahmed says. "Let's go outside and play. Shirzad says he'll meet us down there."

But I am a statue. Frozen solid, I can't seem to switch from War-Ali to War-Is-Over-Ali like *that*. I just can't.

Then Ahmed throws the ball, and I automatically lift my knee and bounce the ball in the air.

It feels good. I bounce the ball onto the other knee.

"Race you!" Ahmed yells and takes off running. I catch the ball in my hands and chase my little brother out the front door and into the blazing sun. I automatically look up to see if there are warplanes before I realize . . . *I don't have to anymore.*

As I kick the ball back and forth with Ahmed, I look

around. In our neighborhood, nobody would know that we have just been in a war. Not one house has been hit. Yet on the radio, we heard about catastrophic damage all over Iraq.

I can't help but think, *Why us? Why are we so lucky?*

Shirzad comes out of the house. Wordlessly, he joins us. I kick the ball around with both my brothers. I start to feel loose. It's easy to lose myself in the rhythm . . . Kick . . . Pass . . . Kick . . . Pass . . .

Then I see my friend Mustafa coming toward us.

"Mustafa!" I shout. "Come play!"

Ahmed kicks the ball, but I let it pass right by me. Mustafa has gotten near enough for me to see his face. I'm ashamed of myself; I hadn't given a thought to my friend.

"Your father?" I ask.

"Not back yet," Mustafa says.

I focus on the word *yet*.

"He'll probably show up any time," I reassure him. Ahmed goes to retrieve the runaway ball.

"Yes." Mustafa nods and tries to smile. "Not know-ing . . . It's hard."

Just then, Shireen comes running out into the street.

"Boys!" she hollers. "Baba says to come in before he has to go to work!"

"Your father is back?" Mustafa says.

"He showed up earlier today," I say.

"That's great, dude!" Mustafa looks genuinely happy for

155

me. I'm reminded of an Iraqi proverb — "You will discover your true friends in moments of crisis."

"Want to come in?" I ask.

"No, thanks," Mustafa says. "My grandmother wants me right back. I don't want to give her anything more to worry about."

I hold out my hand, and we shake. Mustafa heads off down the street, and I follow my siblings into the house.

My parents are right there, in the front hallway. Baba is wearing his medic uniform.

"I'm going to the hospital," he says.

"I don't want you to go, Baba!" Shireen wraps her arms around his legs.

"I know, my little girl," my father says. "But there are many injured people who need my help."

"But what if Saddam Hussein starts another war?" Shireen cries.

We are all quiet for a moment.

"Come on, Shireen," I say. I take her hands and peel her off my father. "There's no war now. And if another one comes, we'll get through it. Together."

"Ali is right," Mama says. "Now come, Shireen, let's see what we can make for supper. Baba brought home some kindling to light the oven. I think we have a bit of grains left for lavash." They head to the kitchen.

"I'll go collect some dates from the tree!" says Ahmed, rushing out the door.

"We'll take care of things here, Baba," says Shirzad.

My father picks up his medical bag and says quietly, to just the two of us, "You boys stay close to home. There are many people in Basra who are angry and upset. There may be trouble in the streets."

"Yes, sir," Shirzad and I say together. We watch our father leave.

"I'm going to my room," my brother says. "Now that it's *mine* again. This morning I stepped on one of Ahmed's army men, and I found a baby doll wedged between the wall and my bed."

I laugh and follow Shirzad up the stairs, taking them two at a time. When I enter my bedroom, I sigh. *Three of my comics gone, casualties of the war.* But everything else looks the same.

I grab a comic and take it to my bed. I lie down and flip it open. I don't know what will happen to us in the days ahead. In the comics, the good guys always win. In real life? It's not always so obvious who the good guys are. The world may see only Saddam Hussein. But we Iraqis are so much more than that.

Whatever happens next, as my father says, we'll get through it together.

THIRTY-TWO

FOURTEEN YEARS LATER

I CAN'T ESCAPE HIS EYES.

Saddam Hussein is looking at me. Saddam Hussein, the former president of Iraq, the Butcher of Baghdad, the man responsible for the deaths of millions of his own people. My own people.

I am falling back in time. Back to when I was a boy whose world seemed nearly always to be at war. Where people were terrorized and tortured and starved and gassed . . .

I take a deep breath and remind myself that I am no longer that boy. I am now a grown man, here in Iraq, with an important job working for the American State Department. I am part of a team in the Iraqi High Tribunal that is prosecuting Saddam Hussein for crimes against humanity.

Saddam is sitting in the defendant's cage — an area surrounded by wooden railings. And security. Plenty of security.

But even with the cage and armed guards and justice on my side, I am rattled. When an evil dictator focuses his laser-beam eyes on you, it feels like Satan is staring into your soul.

"I—" I begin to translate Saddam's Arabic speech into English. "I am not going to answer to this so-called court!" My words go into a microphone and up to the second floor, where behind the mirrored windows sit the Americans.

Only Iraqis are allowed in the main courtroom. The Americans who are helping to prosecute Saddam Hussein through democratic procedures stay behind the scenes, watching and listening and advising.

The judge has just told Saddam to stop yelling.

"You are nobody!" Saddam shouts, getting to his feet. "I am the leader of the Iraqi people!"

I translate Saddam's outburst, while thinking, *This man has no remorse! He's crazy!*

Finally Saddam sits down, and the trial continues.

I listen to the witness on the stand speak. He is telling a heart-wrenching story about his family being killed during the chemical attacks. That was the first phase of a genocide campaign called Al-Anfal.

It's difficult, but I keep my composure. I have a job to do.

I translate the witness's words from Kurdish to English so that the Americans can understand.

I am a professional translator. I was hired by the U.S. government to help bring Saddam to some kind of justice, *finally*.

I am twenty-eight years old. It has been quite a few years since Saddam retreated from Kuwait. I spent my teen-age years living with the economic sanctions that were imposed on my country. We remained hungry, powerless, and silenced. All along, however, I kept learning and practicing my English. The language seemed to come instinctively to me, even though I had been unable to leave Iraq to visit America.

And then, in 2003, there was another war, the Second Gulf War. This time, the government of Saddam Hussein was overthrown. But still Saddam was not killed. He went into hiding for many months. Finally he was yanked out of his hiding place, a hole in the ground, which was known as Saddam's spider hole, in his hometown of Tikrik in a raid by U.S. troops. The Saddam they captured looked like a di-sheveled old man with an overgrown gray beard and bloody scrapes.

The Saddam who is in this courtroom is neatly groomed, and dressed in a white-collared shirt and dark suit. And as dictator-like as ever. He smiles, he smirks, he reprimands and shouts when he gets angry or feels insulted. He gives orders.

Except this time, no one is following his orders. He is the prisoner.

The Kurdish witness finishes his testimony. The defense team asks him some questions.

I translate it all.

And then it is time for court to be adjourned for the day.

I watch the Iraqi security guards escort Saddam to the doorway, where they hand him off to the U.S. Marshals Service, a federal law enforcement agency within the U.S. Department of Justice. Saddam will be taken downstairs to his prison cell. He is currently on a hunger strike to protest the trial.

Everyone in Iraq knows about Saddam's hunger strike. Millions of Iraqis are glued to their television sets. The trial is being televised almost live.

I look up at the high ceiling. I can see many of the cameras that are taping the trial. They beam their images to the control room, where a U.S. production company that also films the American Super Bowl works to edit out some faces and names before airing the trial. So the world sees everything on a thirty-minute delay.

Well, not everything. They don't see me—or the other translators. They only hear our voices. If they showed my face, I would be dead. Saddam's supporters—mostly Sunni

Muslims—would consider me a traitor working with the Americans.

When I talk to my family and friends, whom I'm not allowed to see during the trial, they are excited to hear my voice.

I am in the heavily fortified area called the Green Zone. It's mostly secure—except the occasional bomb that gets through from Saddam's supporters outside. Inside are Americans and Iraqis working to give Saddam Hussein a fair and democratic trial.

Many of us are learning how democracy works.

"Ali!" A man's voice reaches me from the courtroom's entryway. "Are you coming?"

I stand up and respond in English.

"Yes, Mr. D. I'm coming."

I head over to the exit. Time to shake off the day. And shake Mr. D.'s hand.

Mr. D is one of three American attorneys who are helping to prosecute Saddam Hussein.

"Good job today," he tells me. He sips a cup of coffee in his right hand as we walk down the hallway.

"Thank you," I say.

"No, really," he says. "That was some pretty intense stuff in there. You translate so fast, but you still manage to convey emotion. Where did you learn English?"

"Television," I say. "Movies."

He laughs.

"Some schooling," I add. "But I always watched and listened to any English I could find."

"Well, it's certainly paid off," says Mr. D.

"Literally," I joke. "Although to be honest, I would do this job even if I didn't get paid. It's something I can be proud of for the rest of my life."

"You're a good translator and a good man," says Mr. D. "But don't tell the State Department that you'd do this for free. They would take you up on it. So you grew up here in Iraq?"

"Yes," I say. "Mostly in Basra, with my family."

"How are they doing?"

"As well as can be expected," I say. "My parents are healthy. My mother teaches mathematics and my father's a dentist.

"I am very fortunate," I continue. "We have all lived through three wars. Most families in Iraq are not so lucky."

Mr. D. drinks the last of his coffee and drops the cup in a nearby receptacle.

We shake hands. The attorney heads toward the gym. I make a stop before going back to my trailer. Into the game room.

Where I beat the previous high score on the retro Ms. Pac-Man arcade game.

"A-L-I," I spell out on the high score board. And I smile.

EPILOGUE

Saddam Hussein was sentenced to death by hanging after he was convicted of crimes against humanity by the Iraqi High Tribunal. He was executed on Saturday, December 30, 2006.

After the trial, Ali returned to Basra, his hometown. In 2008, with help from Mr. D., one of the prosecuting attorneys in the trial of Saddam Hussein, Ali moved to the United States, and his siblings followed in 2009.

Ali moved to Columbus, Ohio. One night, he had dinner with Mr. D. and his family, including Mr. D's sister-in-law, Jennifer Roy, who later became Ali's coauthor in writing this story.

On November 12, 2013, Ali Fadhil became a citizen of the United States of America.

ACKNOWLEDGMENTS

Thank you to Ali Fadhil, a true ambassador and hero.

Thank you to my twin sister, the author Julia DeVillers, and to David DeVillers for connecting me to Ali and giving me the opportunity to tell this story.

Thank you to my amazing editor, Elizabeth Bewley, and the entire team at HMH. Thank you to designer Sharismar Rodriguez and illustrator Patrick Leger for the book's stunning cover.

Thank you to my patient and brilliant agent, Alyssa Eisner Henkin at Trident Media.

Thanks to my family—my mother, Robin Rozines; Sylvia Perlmutter Rozines; Greg Roy; Quinn DeVillers; Jack DeVillers; Gwen Rudnick.

Thank you to Jeff Walter and the Walter family. Also thanks to my friends Sharon Aibel, Julie Tellstone, and Kelly Stiles.

And a special thank-you to my indispensable son, Adam Roy.

—Jennifer Roy

Thank you to Jennifer Roy for being flexible and having patience when I took forever to answer your questions.

Thank you to David DeVillers and his family. David: You brought a tyrant to justice. Not a lot of people get to claim that.

Thank you to Lieutenant Colonel Hugh McNeely (U.S. Army, Ret.): You taught me that everyone belongs here.

Thank you to my late cousin Sameer, who gave the ultimate sacrifice while fighting ISIS. You are not forgotten.

—Ali Fadhil